EX LIBRIS

VINTAGE CLASSICS

LES ENFANTS TERRIBLES

Jean Cocteau (1889-1963) – poet, novelist, dramatist, artist, musician, choreographer, film-maker, and actor – was one of the most talented Frenchmen of the twentieth century and a leading figure in the Surrealist movement. In addition to his popular novel *Les Enfants Terribles* (1929), he is best remembered in the English-speaking world for the films, *La Belle et La Bête* and *Orphée* (1950) and perhaps his play *La Machine infernale* (1934).

Rosamond Lehmann, who died in 1990, in addition to being a fine translator, was a highly acclaimed novelist, whose works include *Invitation to the Waltz* and *The Echoing Grove*.

JEAN COCTEAU

Les Enfants Terribles

TRANSLATED FROM THE FRENCH BY
Rosamond Lehmann

WITH ILLUSTRATIONS BY THE AUTHOR

VINTAGE BOOKS
London

Published by Vintage 2011

4 6 8 10 9 7 5

First published in France by Grasset in 1929

This translation first published in Great Britain by Harvill in 1955
First published by Vintage in 2003

Vintage
Random House, 20 Vauxhall Bridge Road,
London SW1V 2SA
www.vintage-books.co.uk

Addresses for companies within The Random House Group Limited
can be found at: www.randomhouse.co.uk/offices.htm

The Random House Group Limited Reg. No. 954009

A CIP catalogue record for this book
is available from the British Library

ISBN 9780099561378

The Random House Group Limited supports The Forest Stewardship Council®
(FSC®), the leading international forest-certification organisation. Our books
carrying the FSC label are printed on FSC®-certified paper. FSC is the only
forest-certification scheme supported by the leading environmental organisations,
including Greenpeace. Our paper procurement policy can be found at

Printed and bound in Great Britain by
CPI Group (UK) Ltd, Croydon, CR0 4YY

LES ENFANTS
TERRIBLES

PART ONE

T HAT PORTION OF OLD PARIS known as the Cité Monthiers
is bounded on the one side by the rue de Clichy, on the other
by the rue d'Amsterdam. Should you choose to approach it from
the rue de Clichy, you would come to a pair of wrought iron gates:
but if you were to come by way of the rue d'Amsterdam, you would
reach another entrance, open day and night, and giving access,
first to a block of tenements, and then to the courtyard proper, an
oblong court containing a row of small private dwellings secretively
disposed beneath the flat towering walls of the structure. Clearly
these little houses must be the abode of artists. The windows are
blind, covered with photographers' drapes, but it is comparatively
easy to guess what they conceal: rooms chock-a-block with weapons
and lengths of brocade, with canvases depicting basketfuls of
cats, or the families of Bolivian diplomats. Here dwells the Master,
illustrious, unacknowledged, well-nigh prostrated by the weight of
his public honours and commissions, with all this dumb provincial
stronghold to seal him from disturbance.

Twice a day, however, at half past ten in the morning and four o'clock in the afternoon, the silence is shattered by a sound of tumult. The doors of the little Lycée Condorcet, opposite number 72b rue d'Amsterdam, open, and a horde of schoolboys emerges to occupy the Cité and set up their headquarters. Thus it has re-assumed a sort of medieval character – something in the nature of a Court of Love, a Wonder Fair, an Athletes' Stadium, a Stamp Exchange; also a gangsters' tribune cum place of public execution; also a breeding ground for rags – rags to be hatched out finally in class, after long incubation, before the incredulous eyes of the authorities. Terrors they are, these lads, and no mistake – the terrors of the Fifth. A year from now, having become the Fourth, they will have shaken the dust of the rue d'Amsterdam from their shoes and swaggered into the rue Caumartin with their four books bound with a strap and a square of felt in lieu of a satchel.

But now they are in the Fifth, where the tenebrous instincts of childhood still predominate: animal, vegetable instincts, almost indefinable because they operate in regions below conscious memory, and vanish without trace, like some of childhood's griefs; and also because children stop talking when grown-ups draw nigh. They stop talking, they take on the aspect of beings of a different order of creation – conjuring themselves at will an instantaneous coat of bristles or assuming the bland passivity of some form of plant life. Their rites are obscure, inexorably secret; calling, we know, for infinite cunning, for ordeal by fear and torture; requiring victims, summary executions, human sacrifices. The particular mysteries are impenetrable, the faithful speak a cryptic tongue; even if we were to chance to overhear unseen, we would be none the wiser. Their trade is all in postage stamps and marbles. Their tribute goes to swell the pockets of the demi-gods and leaders; the mutter of conspiracy is shrouded in a deafening din. Should one of that tribe of prosperous, hermetically preserved artists happen to pull the cord that works those drapes across his window, I doubt if the spectacle thereby revealed to him would strike him as copy for any of his favourite subjects: nothing he could use to make a pretty picture with a title such as *Little Black Sweeps at Play in a White World*; or *Hot Cockles*; or *Merry Wee Rascals*.

There was snow that evening. The snow had gone on falling steadily since yesterday, thereby radically altering the original design. The Cité had withdrawn in Time; the snow seemed no longer to be impartially distributed over the whole warm living earth, but to be dropping, piling only upon this one isolated spot.

The hard muddy ground had already been smashed, churned up, crushed, stamped into slides by children on their way to school. The soiled snow made ruts along the gutter. But the snow had also become the snow on porches, steps, and house-fronts: featherweight packages, mats, cornices, odds and ends of wadding, ethereal yet crystallized, seemed, instead of blurring the outlines of the stone, to quicken it, to imbue it with a kind of presage.

Gleaming with the soft effulgence of a luminous dial, the snow's incandescence, self-engendered, reached inward to probe the very soul of luxury and draw it forth through stone till it was visible, till it was that fabric magically upholstering the Cité, shrinking it and transforming it into a phantom drawing-room.

[5]

Seen from below, the prospect had less to recommend it. The street lamps shed a feeble light upon what looked like a deserted battlefield. Frost-flayed, the ground had split, was broken up into fissured blocks, like crazy pavement. In front of every gully-hole, a stack of grimy snow stood ominous, a potential ambush; the gas-jets flickered in a villainous north-easter; and the dark holes and corners already hid their dead.

Viewed from this angle, the illusion produced was altogether different. Houses were no longer boxes in some legendary theatre but houses deliberately blacked out, barricaded by their occupants to hinder the enemy's advance.

In fact the entire Cité had lost its civic status, its character of open mart, fair-ground, and place of execution. The blizzard had commandeered it totally, imposed upon it a specifically military role, a particular strategic function. By ten minutes past four, the operation had developed to the point where none could venture from the porch without incurring risk. Beneath that porch the reservists were assembled, their numbers swollen by the newcomers who continued to arrive singly or two by two.

"Seen Dargelos?"

"Yes . . . No . . . I don't know."

This reply came from one of two youths engaged in bringing in one of the first casualties. He had a handkerchief tied round his knee and was hopping along between them and clinging to their shoulders.

The question had come from a boy with a pale face and melancholy eyes – the eyes of a cripple. He walked with a limp, and his long cloak hung oddly, as if concealing some deformity, some strange protuberance or hump. But nearing a corner piled with school haversacks, he suddenly flung his cloak back, exposing the nature of his disability: not a growth, but a heavy satchel eccentrically balanced on one hip. He dropped it, ceased to be a cripple; the eyes, however, did not alter.

He advanced towards the battle.

To the right, where the footpath joined the arcade, a prisoner was being subjected to interrogation. By the spasmodic flaring of a gas lamp he could be seen to be a small boy with his back against the wall, hemmed in by his captors, a group of four. One of these, a senior boy, was squatting between his legs and twisting his ears, to the accompaniment of a series of hideous facial contortions. By way of crowning horror, the monstrous ever-changing mask confronting the prisoner's was dumb. Weeping, he sought to close his eyes, to avert his head. But every time he struggled, his torturer seized a fistful of grey snow and scrubbed his ears with it.

Circumnavigating the group, threading a path through shot and shell, the pale boy went on his way.

He was looking for Dargelos, whom he loved.

It was the worse for him because he was condemned to love without forewarning of love's nature. His sickness was unremitting and incurable — a state of desire, chaste, innocent of aim or name.

Dargelos was the Lycée's star performer. He throve on popular support and equally on opposition. At the mere sight of those dishevelled locks of his, those scarred and gory knees, that coat with its enthralling pockets, the pale boy lost his head.

The battle gives him courage. He will run, he will seek out Dargelos, fight shoulder to shoulder by his side, defend him, show him what mettle he is made of.

The snow went flying, bursting against cloaks, spattering the walls with stars. Here and there, some fragmentary image stood out in stereoscopic detail between one blindness and the next; a gaping mouth in a red face; a hand pointing — at whom? in what direction? . . . It is at him, none other, that the hand is pointing: he staggers, his pale lips open to frame a shout. He had discerned a figure, one of the god's acolytes, standing on some front door steps. It is he, this acolyte, who compasses his doom. "Darg . . ." His cry is cut off short; the snowball comes crashing on his mouth, his jaws are stuffed with snow, his tongue is paralysed. He has just time to see the laughter, and within the laughter, surrounded by his staff, a form, the form of Dargelos, crowned with blazing cheeks and tumbled hair, rearing itself up with a tremendous gesture.

A blow strikes him full on the breast. A heavy blow. A marble-fisted blow. A marble-hearted blow. His mind fades out, surmising Dargelos upon a kind of dais, supernaturally lit; the arm of Dargelos nerveless, dropping down.

He lay prostrate on the ground. A stream of blood flowed from his mouth, besmearing chin and cheek and soaking into the snow. Whistles rang out. Next moment the Cité was deserted. Only a few remained beside the body, not to succour it but to observe the blood

with avid curiosity. Of these, one or two soon made off, not liking the look of things, shrugging, wagging their heads portentously; others made a dive for their satchels and skidded away. The group containing Dargelos remained upon the steps, immobilized. At length authority appeared in the shape of the proctor and the college porter and headed by a boy, Gérard, whom Paul had hailed upon entering the battle, and who had run to fetch them after having witnessed the disaster. Between them the two men took up the body; the proctor turned to scan the shadows.

"Is that you, Dargelos?"

"Yes, Sir."

"Follow me."

The procession started.

Great are the prerogatives of beauty, subduing even those not consciously aware of it. Dargelos was a favourite with the masters. The proctor felt the whole baffling business to be excessively annoying.

They bore the victim into the porter's lodge, where the kindly porter's wife did her best to bathe him and restore him.

Dargelos stood in the doorway, backed by a throng of curious faces. Gérard knelt beside his friend, tearfully clasping his hand.

"Tell me what happened, Dargelos," said the proctor.

"There's nothing to tell, Sir. Some of the chaps were chucking snowballs. I chucked one at him. It must have been a jolly hard one. It hit him smack in the chest and he went 'Ho!' and fell down. At first I thought his nose was bleeding from another snowball that had hit him in the face."

[10]

"A snowball wouldn't crack a person's ribs."

"Sir, Sir!" cried the boy who answered to the name of Gérard. "He put a stone inside that snowball."

"Is that true?" inquired the proctor.

Dargelos shrugged his shoulders.

"Haven't you anything to say?"

"What's the use . . . Look, he's opening his eyes. You'd better ask him."

The victim was beginning to show signs of life. Gérard slipped an arm under his head and he lay back against it.

"How are you feeling?"

"Sorry . . ."

"There's no need to apologize. You're ill, you fainted."

"I remember now."

"Have you any idea what made you faint?"

"A snowball hit me in the chest."

"A snowball? Why should that make you faint?"

"It's the only thing that hit me."

"Your friend has given me to understand that this particular snowball had a stone in it."

The patient saw Dargelos shrug his shoulders.

"Gérard must he cracked," he said. "You're cracked. It was just an ordinary snowball. I was running, I expect I sort of blew up."

The proctor breathed a sigh of relief.

Dargelos seemed about to take his leave, then changed his mind and advanced a few paces in the direction of the victim. But when he reached the porter's counter, on which were displayed such goods as ink, sweets, pen-holders, he stopped short, pulled a couple of pence from his pocket, flung them down, picked up a twist of liquorice – the kind so popular with boys, that looks like bootlaces – crossed the hall, raised one hand in a sort of military salute, and disappeared.

The proctor had already called a cab, intending to see the patient home, but Gérard objected that it was unnecessary. He declared that the sight of the proctor would alarm the family, and that he himself would be his escort.

"Anyway," he added, "he's much better now – you can see."

The proctor needed little persuasion. It was snowing hard. The lad's home was in the rue Montmartre.

Having seen them into the cab and observed Gérard in the act of removing his cloak and woollen muffler to wrap them round his friend, the proctor concluded that he was justified in washing his hands of further responsibility.

T HE WHEELS TURNED SLOWLY on the slippery road.
Huddled in one corner, Gérard gazed at the head beside him, so
pale it seemed to make the further corner luminous, and bobbing
forlornly with the convulsive bobbing of the cab. The closed eyelids
were barely visible, the nostrils and lips a shadow merely, still
flecked with crusts of blood. He murmured: "Paul . . ."

Paul heard; but he was sunk in such leaden lassitude that he
could not move his tongue. He slid a hand out of his rugs and
wrappings and put it over Gérard's.

A child's reaction to this type of calamity is twofold and extreme.
Not knowing how deeply, powerfully, life drops anchor into its
vast sources of recuperation, he is bound to envisage, at once, the
very worst; yet at the same time, because of his inability to imagine
death, the worst remains totally unreal to him.

Gérard went on repeating: "Paul's dying, Paul's going to die";
but he did not believe it. Paul's death would be part of the dream,
a dream of snow, of journeying forever. For though he loved Paul

as Paul loved Dargelos, it was by being weak, not strong, that Paul had subjugated him. Dargelos was the flame that drew Paul's tranced obsessive gaze; he, Gérard, who was strong and just, must therefore be Paul's guardian, must watch him surreptitiously, save him each time he seemed about to singe his wings. What a fool he'd been on the porch! . . . pretending not to notice that Paul was looking for Dargelos, telling himself he'd jolly well teach Paul a lesson . . . The same compulsion that had hurled the infatuated Paul towards the fray had pinned, transfixed him, Gérard, to the spot. From afar he had seen Paul drop, lie bleeding, senseless, with something in his attitude . . . in the kind of attitude that seems to warn the frivolous spectator to keep his distance. Then, not daring to approach for fear Dargelos and his gang would keep him away from the authorities, he had taken to his heels and run for help.

But now once more the customary rhythm was re-establishing its sway; once more he was at his post, watching over Paul. Now he was bearing him away. He was soaring into a dream-world of transcendent ecstasy. The soundless wheels beneath him, the glitter of the street lamps, combined with his sense of dedication to weave a magic spell. Paul's weakness seemed to him to turn to stone, to acquire concrete and finite dimensions, and he felt that, in bearing it, he had found a cause worthy of his strength.

Suddenly it struck him that he had accused Dargelos. Spite had prompted him to perpetrate an act of malice and injustice. He remembered the porter's lodge, that shoulder shrugged in scorn, Paul's blue reproachful eye, Paul's superhuman effort to declare "You're cracked!" – and thus to acquit the culprit. He felt uneasy, tried to dismiss the matter, telling himself by way of self-excuse that a snowball in Dargelos's iron hands could be a weapon potentially more lethal than his own nine-bladed penknife. Surely Paul would forget the incident. At all costs the true world of childhood must prevail, must be restored; that world whose momentous, heroic, mysterious quality is fed on airy nothings, whose substance is so ill-fitted to withstand the brutal touch of adult inquisition.

On went the cab, jogging through the open firmament. Stars came towards it, splintering the dim shower-whipped windows with fiery particles of light.

Suddenly a cry was heard, two plaintive notes. Piercing, human they swelled, inhuman; the panes rattled; the fire brigade went storming by. Through chinks in the frosted glass Gérard could discern the bases of the engines, the scarlet ladders, the firemen standing motionless, gold-helmeted in their niches, like allegorical figures on a monument. A ruddy flicker danced across Paul's face. Gérard fancied him reviving. But the last of the whirlwind passed, leaving him death-pale as before. It was then that Gérard noticed that the hand in his own was warm, and understood that his ability to play the Game stemmed from this link with living warmth.

The word "Game" was by no means accurate, but it was the term which Paul had selected to denote that state of semi-consciousness in which children float immersed. Of this Game he was past master. Lord of space and time, dweller in the twilit fringes between light and darkness, fisher in the confluent pools of truth and fantasy, he had built himself a kingdom in his classroom, sat at his desk enthroned while Dargelos bowed in homage, obedient to his will.

"Can he be playing the Game?" thought Gérard, clasping Paul's warm hand, staring intently at the face supine in its corner.

Without Paul's presence, this cab would have been nothing but a cab, the snow no more than snow, the lamps mere lamps, this return journey a humdrum routine affair. Too homespun by nature for any self-induced delirium, Gérard was totally possessed by Paul, whose spell had finally pervaded his entire consciousness. Instead of learning grammar, sums, geography, natural history, he had been made free of such a sphere of sleep as wafts the waking dreamer past danger of recall, and restores to things their veritable meaning. The opium hidden in their desks – in the shape of pieces of chewed india-rubber, broken pen-holders – provided these infant addicts with a drug as potent as any drowsy syrup of the East.

Could Paul be playing the Game?

Gérard knew better than to suppose that a mere passing fleet of fire engines would have disturbed him in this play.

He tried to pick up its tenuous threads again, but it was too late. The cab had come to a halt in front of the door.

Paul roused himself.

"Shall I get help?" asked Gérard. No need. If Gérard would give him a hand he could manage the stairs . . . if Gérard would hang on to his satchel . . .

Gérard lifted out the satchel, clasped Paul round the waist, and with Paul's left arm slung round his neck, started to mount the stairs. On the first landing he stopped, deposited his precious burden upon a derelict settee with springs and stuffing bulging through green plush upholstery. He went towards the right-hand door and touched the bell.

Footsteps sounded; ceased. Silence.

"Elisabeth!" Still not a sound.

"Elisabeth!" called Gérard in an urgent whisper. "Open the door. It's us."

"I shan't open the door!" remarked a small stubborn voice from the other side of it. "I'm sick to death of boys. Turning up at this hour of the night — you must be mad. I'm fed up with you."

"Lisbeth, do open the door," insisted Gérard. "Hurry up, Paul's ill."

There was a pause; then the door opened just a fraction and the voice was heard to say:

"Ill? You can't catch me. I know you're only trying to make me let you in. You're telling an untruth, aren't you? Are you?"

"Paul's ill, I tell you, do buck up. He's on the settee, he's shivering."

The door opened wide to reveal a girl of sixteen, with a strong physical resemblance to Paul. She had the same blue eyes shadowed by dark lashes, the same pallor of complexion. But whereas the lines of his face betrayed a certain weakness of comparison, hers, two years older, beneath soft curling hair, had already ceased to be a sketch for the finished portrait, was already groping for its organic principle and racing, dishevelled, to overtake its beauty.

It was her whiteness that loomed first against the hall's dark background; that, and the pale blot of the kitchen apron, far too long for her, tied round her waist.

[17]

It was true then, not a sell, she told herself, struck dumb. With Gérard's assistance she lifted Paul and helped him in — a reeling figure, his head sunk on his chest. The moment they were in the hall, Gérard started to make a statement.

"Idiot," she hissed. "There you go, as usual — trust you to make a hash of it. *Must* you shout? *Can't* you be quiet? Do you want Mother to hear?"

They crossed the dining-room, describing a circle round the table to reach the children's bedroom on the right.

Here the furniture consisted of two diminutive beds, a chest of drawers, three chairs, and a mantelpiece. A door between the beds gave access to the kitchen-dressing-room which boasted a second entrance, from the hall.

It was a bedroom to startle an unaccustomed eye. But for the beds, it would have seemed a lumber room. The floor was strewn with empty boxes, with towels and various articles of underwear; apart from these, one threadbare rug adorned it. A plaster bust, its features emphasized by inked-in eyes and a moustache, occupied a central position on the mantelpiece. Every available inch of wall space was stuck with drawing-pins impaling sheets of newspaper, pages torn out of magazines, programmes, photographs of film stars, murderers, boxers.

Elisabeth led the way, swearing, forcing a path between the boxes by means of violent kicks delivered left and right. At length they stretched him on his bed, among a tumbled heap of books. Then Gérard told his tale.

"It's the limit!" burst out Elisabeth. "Here am I, tied hand and foot to my poor sick mother, while you go snowballing. A precious pair, I must say. My poor sick mother!" she said again, agreeably struck by the phrase and by the sense of dignity it gave her. "I tend my poor mother on her bed of sickness while you disport yourself with snowballs. I bet it was you as usual who made Paul do it, you idiot!"

Gérard held his tongue. He was familiar with the impassioned rhetoric coupled with schoolboy slang the pair affected, as well as with their perpetual state of nervous tension. But he remained shy and could not help being a little upset by it.

"Who'll have to nurse Paul," she went on, "you or me? What are you standing there for, gaping at me?"

"Libbie darling . . ."

"I'm not Libbie, and I'm not your darling. Kindly keep a civil tongue in your head. Besides . . ."

A far-away voice broke in on them.

"Gérard, old chap," Paul muttered. "Don't take any notice of the bitch. It's too boring."

Elisabeth was stung.

"Oh, I'm a bitch, am I? All right, you dirty dogs, I'm through. You can damn well fend for yourself. It's the end. Fancy me bothering about a feeble ass who can't stand up to a harmless little snowball! Look, Gérard," she went on without a break, "watch." She executed a sudden violent high kick that flung her right leg higher than her head. "I've been practising that for weeks." She repeated the performance. "And now, be off! Get a move on."

She pointed to the door.

On the threshold Gérard hesitated.

[19]

"Perhaps . . ." he stammered. "Oughtn't we to get a doctor . . ."

She swung a leg up.

"A doctor? I was so hoping to have the benefit of your advice. What it is to be brainy! Perhaps I might humbly beg to mention the doctor's coming to see Mummy at seven o'clock and I thought of getting him to look at Paul. Go on now, skedaddle!" Then, as Gérard still hovered uncertainly, she added: "Or are you a medical man, by any chance? Oh, you're not? Then leave this house. *Will* you be off?"

She stamped her foot, her eye flashed, steely. Beating a hasty retreat backwards through the dark dining-room he knocked a chair over.

"Idiot! Idiot!" she repeated. "Don't pick it up, you'd only knock another over. Make haste, for heaven's sake! And mind you don't bang the door."

On the landing, Gérard remembered that the cab was still waiting and that he had not a penny in his pockets. He dared not ring again. She would take no notice; or if she did, she would be expecting to see the doctor, and flay him, Gérard, with her tongue.

He lived with his guardian, whose nephew he was, in the rue Lafitte. He decided to take the cab on home, then explain the situation to his uncle and persuade him to settle the whole bill.

He sank into Paul's corner of the cab; deliberately he let his head loll back, surrendered, as Paul's had been, to the jolting springs. He made no attempt to play the Game; he was feeling wretched. His fabulous journey was over, he was back now in the discomfiting climate of Elisabeth and Paul. She had shattered his dream of Paul in his pure weakness, stabbed him awake with reminders of his selfish whims. Paul in his relationship to Dargelos, Paul victim, overthrown, was not that Paul to whom he, Gérard, was in thrall.

There had been something of perversion, almost of necrophily, in the delicious pleasures of that journey with the unconscious youth: not that he envisaged it in such crude psychopathic terms. All the same he realized that Paul's swoon, the falling snow, had contributed to an illusion. Paul had been absent, dead. Only the ruddy glow cast by the flying fire engines had given him a counterfeit life. He understood Elisabeth — knew, of course, that her affection for him was simply an extension of her worship of her brother. Oh yes, he was their friend, had witnessed their transports of immoderate love, the stormy glances they exchanged, the clash of their conflicting fantasies and their malicious tongues. He lay back soberly in the cab and let his head roll to and fro and felt the draught cold on the back of his neck and set about reducing his world to commonsense proportions. But a rational approach had its disadvantages as well as its rewards. If on the one hand it enabled him to discern a tender heart beneath her outward harshness, on the other it forced him to recognize Paul's seizure for what it was — a real, grown-up fainting-fit, suggesting dire possibilities.

The cab stopped at his front door. Placating the grumbling driver as best he could, he rushed upstairs to find his uncle, who gave his case kindly and prompt attention.

Downstairs again. The road stretched blank as far as eye could see, empty of everything but snow. Presumably the driver had thrown his hand in, picked up another fare willing to settle the amount already on the meter, and driven off. Gérard pocketed his uncle's money. He thought: "I'll keep it and say nothing. I'll use it to buy Elisabeth a present. Then I shall have an excuse to go round and see her and get more news."

Meanwhile, in the rue Montmartre, after the rout of Gérard, Elisabeth was with her mother. The sick woman lay with her eyes shut in a bedroom opening into a shabby drawing-room on the left side of the apartment. Four months ago this woman had been young and vigorous. Then, without warning, paralysis had struck her down; and now she looked like an old woman. She was thirty-five years old and longed for death.

She had been bewitched, spoiled, and finally deserted by her husband. For three years he had gone on treating his family to occasional brief visits, during the course of which — having meanwhile developed cirrhosis of the liver — he would brandish revolvers, threaten suicide, and order them to nurse the master of the house; for the mistress with whom he lived refused this office and kicked him out whenever his attacks occurred. His custom was to go back to her as soon as he felt better. He turned up one day at home, raged, stamped, took to his bed, found himself unable to get up again, and died; thereby bestowing his end upon the wife he had repudiated.

An impulse of rebellion now turned this woman into a mother who neglected her children, took to night clubs, got herself up like a tart, sacked her maid once a week, begged, borrowed indiscriminately.

Elisabeth and Paul had inherited her pallor and her cast of countenance. Their heritage of instability, extravagant caprice, and natural elegance was their paternal portion.

Now, as she lay there, she was thinking to herself, "Why go on living?" The doctor was an old friend, he would keep an eye on the children, see that they did not come to grief. She had become a hopeless liability, a millstone round her daughter's neck, a burden to them all.

"Are you asleep, Mummy?"

"No. Just dozing."

"Paul's strained himself. I've put him to bed. I'll ask the doctor to look at him."

"Is he in pain?"

"He says it hurts when he walks. He sends his love. He's got his newspapers, he's doing some cutting out."

The sick woman sighed, reluctant to pursue the matter. She had the egotism born of suffering, as well as a settled habit of dependence on her daughter.

"What about a maid?"

"I can manage."

Elisabeth went back to her own quarters. She found Paul lying with his face to the wall. Stooping over him she said:

"Are you asleep?"

"Leave me alone."

"Very polite, I'm sure. Charming manners. I suppose you've gone away." (To "go away" was a private term in the Game, i.e. they said: I'm going to go away; I'm going away; I've gone away. To

[23]

disturb a player once this third stage had been accomplished was considered unforgivable.)

"Here am I toiling and slaving while you go away. You're a cad; you're a disgusting cad. Here, hold your foot up, let me take off your shoes. Your feet are frozen. Wait, I'll get you a hot water bottle."

She put his muddy shoes on the mantelpiece beside the bust and vanished into the kitchen. Presently she could be heard lighting the gas. Then she came back and set about undressing Paul. He let out a grunt, but made no further protest, silently complying at intervals with such requests as: "Lift your head"; "Lift your leg"; "Will you kindly stop shamming dead, I'll never get this sleeve off."

As she took off his clothes, she emptied his pockets of their miscellaneous contents: item, an ink-stained handkerchief, item, some bait, item, a few lozenges stuck together with fluff. All these she threw on the floor; the rest of the hoard, consisting of a miniature hand in ivory, a marble, the cap of a fountain-pen, she deposited in one of the drawers of the wardrobe.

Here was the treasure, a treasure impossible to describe because the assortment of miscellaneous objects in the drawer had been so far stripped of their original function, so charged with symbolism, that what remained looked merely like old junk — empty aspirin bottles, metal rings, keys, curling-pins; all worthless rubbish, save to the eye of the initiate.

She filled the bottle, slipped it between the sheets, pulled off his day shirt, skinned him like a rabbit, swore, put on his night shirt; disarmed, as usual, melted almost to tears, by the grace and beauty of his body. She settled him down, tucked him up, then said

[24]

with a little gesture of dismissal: "Go to sleep, silly." After which, summoning a look of maniac concentration, she started to practise a few exercises.

She was startled by the faint ringing of the front door bell; it had been lagged with a cloth to muffle it, and was barely audible. The doctor had come. She flew to meet him, clutching his overcoat to drag him towards Paul's bedside while she poured out explanations.

"Go and get the thermometer and then run along, there's a good girl. You can wait in the drawing-room. I'm going to sound his chest and I always dislike an audience."

Elisabeth crossed the dining-room and went into the drawing-room. Here too the snow had been about its magic work. The room hung in mid-air, miraculously suspended, changed, unfamiliar to the child who stood there, stock still, staring, behind one of the armchairs. The lamplit brightness of the opposite pavement had printed on the ceiling several windows made of squares of shadow and half-shadow curtained with arabesques of light; upon this groundwork the silhou-etted forms of passers-by circled diminished as in a moving fresco.

The mirror, which had begun to come alive, revealing within its depths a spectral figure, motionless, poised midway between floor and cornice, added a further touch of travesty to this aereal dwelling, swept darkly ever and again by the broad headlight of a passing car.

She tried to play the Game, but found she could not. Her heart, aware, like Gérard's, that their private legend would not assimilate the snowball and its consequences, was beating an alarum. Such events belonged to the stark world of fear and doctors, a world of people who run temperatures and catch their deaths. In a flash she saw it all: her mother paralysed, her brother dying, no help in the house, no love, the cupboard bare, cold scraps, dry biscuits nibbled at odd hours, then nothing – a bowl of broth perhaps, left by a neighbour.

Within the framework of their legend, the consumption, in bed, of quantities of barley sugar had become *de rigueur* – a fortifying accompaniment to their ceremonial sessions of quarrelling over books. They read the same books over and over again, snatching them acrimoniously from one another, devouring them with gluttonous indiscretion, aiming to reach satiety, revulsion, and so begin the Game: for this initial stage was integrally designed like every other – beginning with the ritual preparation of the beds, the smoothing, the brushing out of crumbs – to serve the Game's one end and give it wings for flight.

She had gone well away at last when she heard her name called. "Lise!"

It was the doctor, shocking her back into the world of grief. She opened the door.

"Come now," he said, "no need to make such heavy weather of it. He's not dangerously ill. It's serious, mind – but not dangerous. The slightest blow on a weak chest like his . . . No more school – that's out of the question. Rest, rest, and again *rest*. You were quite right to tell your mother it was just a strain – we don't want her worried. You're a sensible girl, I can rely on you. I'd like a word with your maid."

"There isn't a maid any more."

"Capital. I shall be sending a couple of nurses in tomorrow. They'll take turns running the house and doing the shopping. You'll be in charge, of course."

She did not thank him. She was accustomed to miracles and accepted them as part of daily life. She expected them to happen, and they always did.

The doctor paid his routine visit to his other patient, and went away.

Paul slept. Elisabeth kept watch beside him, listening to his breathing, her passionate anger spent, or rather turned to a passionately tender contemplation. Sick and asleep, he was exposed to scrutiny, immune from teasing. She could examine the mauve stains beneath his eyelids, the fullness and forward lift of the upper lip; she could lay her head against the boyish arm. What is this uproar in her ears? Blocking one ear, she strains to listen, hears her own hammering pulses amplifying his. Louder, louder? . . . She panics. Surely if this goes on it must mean death. Wake up! She must wake him up.

"My darling!"

"Mm? What d'you want?" He stretches himself; her haggard face confronts him. "What's the matter? Have you gone nuts?"

"*Me* nuts!"

"Yes, you. What a nuisance you are. Can't you let a chap get a bit of sleep?"

"*Some* people could do with a bit of sleep themselves, but oh dear no! *They* have to listen to the row other people make."

"What row?"

"A bloody awful row."

"Idiot!"

"I was going to tell you something — some very exciting news. But as I'm an idiot, I shan't bother."

He pricked up his ears. Exciting news? . . . But he smelt a rat. He wasn't going to let himself be caught so easily.

"You can keep your old news," he said. "I couldn't care less."

She undressed. Neither of them knew the meaning of embarrassment in the presence of the other. This room they shared was as it were a shell in which they lived, washed, dressed together as naturally as if they were twin halves of a single body.

She put a plate of cold beef, some bananas, and a glass of milk on a chair beside his head; then fetched herself a bottle of ginger-beer and a few sweet biscuits, got into bed, and opened a book. She read, munched on in silence until Paul spoke, suddenly devoured by curiosity, requesting to be told the doctor's verdict; not that this interested him *qua* medical opinion: it was the news — presumably somehow connected with it — that he was angling for.

Elisabeth went on munching, her eyes glued to the page, while she considered her dilemma. She was reluctant to enlighten him; yet a point-blank refusal might be unwise. Finally, she flung at him, on in offhand note: "He said you wouldn't be going back to school."

Paul closed his eyes. Intolerable vistas yawned before him, with Dargelos vanishing down all of them, Dargelos forever elsewhere, irrevocably absent from the future. The pain was too sharp, he cried out:

"Lise!"

[29]

"Well?"

"Lise, I don't feel well."

"What's the matter now?"

She got up, stumbled; one leg had gone to sleep.

"What is it you want?"

"I want . . . I want you to stay by me, near my bed."

The tears streamed down his face. He wept as very young children weep, in a welter of tears and snot, his lower lip pushed forward. She dragged her bed across the kitchen floor, close up to his, got into bed again, reached for his hand across the chair that separated them, and started to stroke it.

"There," she said. "There . . . who's a silly billy? You tell him he's never going back to school, and he boo-hoos. Just think! . . . We needn't ever budge from this room now. We'll have nurses dressed in white, the doctor promised me, and I'll never leave you except to go out for sweets or books."

Still the tears poured down, streaking his drenched wan face and splashing on the pillow.

Puzzled, taken aback, she bit her lip, said:

"Are you in a flap?"

Paul shook his head.

"Are you as keen on lessons as all that?"

"No."

"Then what on earth . . . ? Listen, blast you." She shook him by the arm. "Would you like to play the Game? Do wipe your nose. Look at me. I'm going to hypnotize you."

Dilating her eyes to the utmost she leaned over him.

Paul wept and sobbed. Elisabeth was beginning to feel tired. She wanted to play the Game, to hypnotize him; she longed to comfort him; she would have liked to understand. But sleep was bearing down on her, sweeping her mind with broad dark beams like headlights across snow, obliterating all her efforts.

By the following day the household had been radically transformed and reorganized. Calling at five-thirty with a box containing a posy of artificial Parma violets, Gérard found himself admitted by a trained nurse in a white overall. Elisabeth was greatly taken by the posy.

"Do go and see Paul," she urged him, unequivocally cordial. "I'm busy at the moment – I've got to superintend Mummy's injection."

Washed, with his hair brushed neatly, Paul looked almost blooming. He asked for news from school. The news was shattering.

Dargelos had been summoned that morning by the headmaster for further interrogation. He had lost his temper and answered back in so insolent a fashion that the headmaster had leaped from his armchair and threatened him with his clenched fist. Whereupon Dargelos had pulled a bag of pepper from his pocket and flung the contents full in the headmaster's face.

The consequences had been so instantaneous, so appalling, that the panic-stricken Dargelos had bounded forthwith on to a chair, in the manner of one facing the savage onrush of some cataclysmic flood and making an instinctive bid for safety. From this advantageous position he had witnessed the spectacle of a blind old man tearing at his collar, bellowing, rolling on the table, and displaying every symptom of raving lunacy. This was the scene which had greeted the dumbfounded invigilator when, startled by the sounds of uproar, he had come hurrying to the rescue: a raving madman, and Dargelos perched on his chair, stupefied, just as he had been after throwing the snowball.

The headmaster had been removed to hospital, and Dargelos had been sentenced — not to death, since schoolboys are exempt from the supreme penalty — but to expulsion. He had crossed the courtyard with his head high, with a ferocious scowl; he had shaken hands with no one.

Needless to dwell on Paul's reactions to this shocking story . . . But, since Gérard had been at pains to suppress any tendency to crow, it would clearly be unseemly to parade his anguish. He tried to control himself, but could not; and presently he said:

"Do you know his address?"

"No, old boy, I don't. Chaps like him never let on where they hang out."

"Poor Dargelos! That's that, then. Go and get the photographs."

Gérard found two behind the bust and handed them to Paul. One was a school group showing the whole class ranged according to height, with Paul and Dargelos on the left of the housemaster, squatting side by side. Arms folded, arrogant, posed like a footballer, Dargelos displayed those legs which had so notably contributed to his prestige. The other photograph showed him dressed as Athalie — a role he had set his heart on playing in a recent school performance of *Athalie* in honour of St Charlemagne's Day. Tigerish beneath his veils and tinsel draperies, he looked like some great tragic actress of the late nineteenth century.

The entrance of Elisabeth disrupted a scene of pious reminiscence.

"In with it now, I think, don't you?" said Paul, waving the second photograph.

"What? Where?"

"Into the treasure."

"What's to go into the treasure?"

Her brow darkened. The treasure was holy, not to be trifled with. She was jealous of its sanctity and of her rights in it.

"If you agree," said Paul. "It's the chap who chucked the snowball – his photograph."

"Let me see."

For a long time she studied it in silence.

"He chucked the snowball," went on Paul. "He threw pepper at the headmaster. He's been expelled."

Elisabeth continued to pace up and down, biting her thumbnail, rapt in silent contemplation and debate. Finally, she opened the drawer a fraction, pushed the photograph inside, closed it again.

"It's a bad face," she said. "Mind you don't tire Paul, Giraffe." (This was their pet name for Gérard.) "I must go back to Mummy. I've got to keep an eye on the nurses. It's awfully difficult, you know. They're trying to get the upper hand. I daren't leave them for a moment."

Half in earnest, half in self-derision, she made a histrionic gesture of running her fingers through her hair; then, turning, swept from the room as if manipulating an imaginary train.

THANKS TO THE DOCTOR, the children's lives now conformed to a somewhat less abnormal pattern. They themselves, however, cared nothing for conventional amenities; those they enjoyed were theirs alone, and not of this world. Only Dargelos could have persuaded Paul back to school. With Dargelos cast forth, the Lycée Condorcet had become a prison.

For the rest, Dargelos's prestige was beginning to undergo a subtle change of scale. Far from dwindling, his figure was expanding, beginning to take off into the upper reaches of the Room. Those sunken eyes, those lips, so coarse, that lock of hair, those clumsy hands, those knees and all their scars, were becoming separate stars of one great constellation, spinning, turning, in interstellar vacancy. In short, Dargelos had gone into the treasure to rejoin his photograph. Image and original were identified; the prototype had lost his function. As an abstraction, as the ideal image of a handsome fellow, Dargelos became a valuable property, potent in the magic zone; and thus delivered of him, Paul revelled freely in the sweet delights of sickness and perpetual holiday.

As for the Room, the efforts of the nurses proved unavailing to subdue it. On the contrary, the wilderness spread rapidly, and before long the patient had succeeded in imposing his personal town and landscape upon chaos. Streets wound in and out among the litter, trunks flanked his broad avenues, strewn papers were his lakes, piles of discarded linen were his mountains. All these Elisabeth with a murmur of "Laundress . . . waiting . . ." would pounce on and demolish, rejoicing in the havoc she created, the atmosphere of perpetually impending storm which was the breath of life to both of them.

Gérard called every day, to be greeted with volleys of foul language; which he accepted meekly with a smile. Prolonged familiarity with their technique of welcome had rendered him immune. Indeed, the words flung at him had come almost to caress his ears. Then they would burst into hoots of laughter, comment derisively on his "stiff upper lip", and make a great show of conspiratorial giggling and whispering.

But Gérard had the whole performance taped. Unshaken, tireless in the pursuit of his investigations, he went on combing the Room for traces of some new caprice already under seal of secrecy. Thus one day he came upon these words, printed in soap upon the mirror: *Suicide is a mortal sin*.

Clamorous affirmation, stamped indelibly, but doubtless assumed by the children to be no more visible than a scrawl in water, the slogan – symbolic equivalent, no doubt, of the moustache that

decked the bust — bore witness to some rare lyric mood whose secret none might share.

Then, at some clumsy thrust of Gérard's, Paul would abandon him for worthier quarry and apostrophize his sister, sighing: "Ah, you wait till I've got my own room."

"You wait till I've got mine."

"Fine sort of room that's going to be!"

"Jolly sight better than yours! I say, Giraffe, he's going to have a chandelier . . ."

"Shut up!"

"And a sphinx, Giraffe, he's going to have a plaster sphinx on the mantelpiece and he's going to give his Louis XIV chandelier a coat of paint." She collapsed with laughter.

"Perfectly true, I do intend to have a sphinx and a chandelier. You wouldn't understand, of course, you're too ignorant."

"O.K., I'm off. I shall take a room in the hotel. I've got my bag already packed. I shall go and live in the hotel. He can jolly well look after himself. I simply refuse to live here any more. I've packed my bag. I'm not going to live with the great oaf a moment longer."

The performance ended invariably with Elisabeth sticking out her tongue, raining kicks on the planned chaos of the model city, and storming off. Paul would spit after her retreating back. She would bang the door; was presently to be heard banging other doors.

Paul was subject to occasional brief spells of sleep-walking, whose recurrence, far from alarming his sister, filled her with delight; for they and they alone compelled this nitwit she was saddled with to leave his bed.

The moment she saw a pair of long legs appear and start to move in a certain way, she would become transfixed, intent, holding her breath to watch, while before her paced a living statue, prowling, adroitly manoeuvring, then climbing back into bed and settling down again.

Suddenly their mother died – a shock that stunned them. Thinking her immortal, they had treated her with scant consideration; but nevertheless they loved her. To make matters worse, they felt they were to blame; for she had died all unbeknown to them, while they were quarrelling in her room, the very evening when Paul got up for the first time.

The nurse was in the kitchen. The row degenerated into an exchange of blows; with cheeks aflame, Elisabeth had fled to seek sanctuary beside her mother's chair. She found herself confronted by an unknown woman staring at her with wide open tragic eyes and mouth.

She had been surprised by death, perpetuated in such a pose as death alone conceives of: hands clenched, arms rigid along the chair-arms. The doctor had foreseen that the end would come without warning; but the children, alone, transfixed by this sudden counterfeit, this puppet in place of a live person, this stranger with the mask of a sculptured sage, gazed on it livid, stone-still before its petrified stare, its cry of stone.

*

The haunting image was not soon to fade. A time of bewilderment ensued, of tears and mourning, of Paul's relapse, of words of comfort spoken by the doctor and by Gérard's uncle; a time also of practical support in the shape of a trained nurse. These crises having been surmounted, the children found themselves once more alone together.

Far from bequeathing them a distressful legacy, their mother did much, by her fabulous death, to raise her credit in her children's estimation. It was as if a thunderbolt had forged an image of her, acceptably macabre, entirely unrelated to the person whom they missed. Moreover, in matters of bereavement, creatures so primitive, so uncorrupted, are unaware of social usage. Their reactions are animal, instinctive; and orphaned animals are notoriously cynical in their approach to death. The vanished mother is not mourned for long – once gone, never to return, from her accustomed place, her absence is accepted. And yet, by virtue of her one last freakish stroke, she was to manage, after all, to impress herself upon the memory of her children. Besides, the Room craved marvels. This death of hers, indubitably a marvel, made her a sarcophagus, a gothic monument, enshrined her in the Room; was duly to translate her into the eternity of dreams, into their magic heaven, with pride of place.

P AUL'S RELAPSE WAS DANGEROUS; prolonged. Mariette the nurse, a dedicated character, took charge. The doctor had become a martinet. He insisted upon plenty of rest, plenty of nourishment, no excitement. He made himself financially responsible, visited them regularly with strict injunctions, came back again to see that they were carried out.

At first Elisabeth had been recalcitrant, aggressive, but before long she found herself unable to resist Mariette's plump rosy face, her silver curls, and her unshakable if sorely tried devotion. She was an unlettered peasant, whose inmost heart was given to a grandson in her native Brittany. Thus, love had taught her to decipher the mysteries of childhood.

The average upright citizen would have found Paul and Elisabeth preposterous; would doubtless have invoked their tainted heredity — one aunt insane, an alcoholic father — to help explain them. Preposterous they were, indeed; so is a rose; so are the solemn arguments of average upright citizens. But in her perfect simplicity Mariette grasped the inapprehensible. The climate of innocence was one in which she felt herself at home. She had no wish to analyse it. She discerned in the Room a transparency of atmosphere too pure, too vital to harbour any germ of what was base or vile; a spiritual altitude beyond contamination. She sheltered them beneath her wing with an instinctive maternal response to the demands of genius, and with an artless wisdom that enabled her to respect, as if by divination, the creative genius at work within the Room. For it was indubitably a masterpiece these children were creating; a masterpiece devoid of intellectual content, devoid — this was the miracle — of any worldly aim; the masterpiece of their own being.

Paul, one need scarcely add, wasted no opportunity of manipulating the thermometer and generally exploiting his ill-health. Abuse from Elisabeth produced no reaction whatsoever: he remained impassive, mute.

She sulked, she withdrew into scornful silence. When this palled, she gave it up, and presented herself in the brand new role of shrew turned ministering angel. Tiptoeing about, speaking just above a whisper, opening and closing doors with infinite discretion, prodigal of self-giving, she ministered to Paul in the spirit of one compassionately dedicated to the care of feeble-minded paupers.

She decided to become a hospital nurse; to take lessons in nursing from Mariette. She shut herself up for hours on end with the moustachioed plaster bust; also some torn shirts, cotton-wool, gauze, and safety-pins. Coming into the unlit room, Mariette would see the bust staring at her in the darkness from some unexpected angle, ghastly, haggard, its head swathed in bandages. Each time she saw it she nearly died of fright.

The doctor congratulated Elisabeth upon a transformation which seemed to him miraculous, no less.

And she continued to sustain it; gradually, stubbornly, to make a substance of her seeming. For nothing in our hero and our heroine was conscious; no notion crossed them, even faintly, of the external impression they produced. They lived their dream, their Room, fancying they loathed what they adored. They went on planning to have separate rooms, but it occurred to neither of them to move into the empty one. To be more accurate, Elisabeth had given the project one hour's consideration; but the memory of the dead woman, now sublimated in the Room itself, was more frightening in that bedroom. She told herself she could not leave the patient, and remained with him.

On top of everything else, Paul now had growing pains. Penned in the sentry-box he had constructed out of pillows, he complained of cramps. Elisabeth would take no notice, would steal away, finger on lip, with the gait and tread of a young man creeping home stealthily in the small hours, shoes in hand; whereupon, with a shrug, Paul would resume the Game.

In April he got up. He could no longer stand. His new-born legs collapsed beneath him. To Elisabeth's extreme annoyance, he was now half a head taller than herself: she retaliated by adopting the demeanour of a saint, rushing to support him, to lower him into his chair, covering him with wraps – in short, reducing him to the status of a gouty old dotard.

Although disconcerted by this new thrust of hers, he controlled an overwhelming impulse to fight back, and took no notice. Matched against her in a perpetual duel from birth, he had acquired tactical sagacity. Besides, he was too lazy to be otherwise than passive. Elisabeth seethed inwardly. Once more the fight was on, the balance was redressed, the stakes were equal.

By imperceptible stages, Elisabeth began to take the place in Gérard's heart once occupied by Paul. Not to be with her was almost unendurable. Strictly speaking, it had been the house in the rue Montmartre, it had been Paul and Elisabeth that he had adored in Paul. But now, inevitably, the spotlight had swung away from Paul to illumine a figure putting off childhood and slipping into her young girlhood, leaving the time of boys' derision for the time of boys' desire.

Cut off by doctor's orders from the sickroom, he racked his brains for other means of access, and finally managed to persuade his uncle to take Lise and the invalid away to the seaside. This uncle was a wealthy, genial bachelor, overwhelmed with executive meetings and business responsibilities. He had adopted Gérard – son of a widowed sister who had died in giving him birth – and had assured his future by a generous provision in his will. The idea of a holiday appealed to him; he needed a little rest.

Instead of the scathing reception he had expected, Gérard found himself welcomed by a Saint and a Simpleton, and showered with thanks and blessings. What could they be up to? Were they preparing to launch a fresh attack? While pondering these matters, he intercepted an exchange of signals – one flash through a lowered saintly lid, one quiver of the nostril from the Simpleton – and realized the Game was on. These manifestations were not aimed at him: he had merely dropped in upon a performance already in full swing. Another cycle had begun: he had only to adapt himself to an unfamiliar rhythm and thank his stars for granting propitious omens for their journey. Such courteous well-bred guests could hardly fail to please their host-to-be.

They did not fail. In fact, his uncle was quite bowled over by the beautiful dispositions of these ill-reputed friends.

Elisabeth set herself to charm him.

"You know," she simpered, "my little brother's rather shy . . ."

Gérard's attentive ear caught a muttered "Bitch!" from little brother; but nothing else escaped his lips.

In the train they had to make heroic efforts to preserve an appearance of composure. Totally unsophisticated as they were, a *wagon-lit* represented for them the height of luxury; but their natural good breeding and sense of style enabled them to seem perfectly at ease.

Inevitably, the sleeper conjured up the Room, and the same thought flashed into the minds of both: "We shall be having two rooms and two beds at the hotel."

Paul lay motionless. Between lowered lids, Elisabeth traced the outline of his profile, faintly luminous under the blue night-light. In the course of many a deep and stealthy vigil she had become aware of an endemic sloth in him, and of the fact that since his recent therapeutic isolation he was gradually succumbing to it. His rather receding chin annoyed her; her own chin was pronounced. She was apt to say: "Paul, your chin!" in the manner of a maternal "Stand up straight!" or "Elbows off the table!" He would crack back at her with some obscenity, but all the same she had caught him more than once before the mirror, busy manipulating the angle of his jaw.

The year before, she had gone through a phase of sleeping with a clothes-peg on her nose, with the notion of cultivating a Greek profile. Paul had taken to sleeping half-strangled by a tight elastic band; but discouraged by the red mark it left, he renounced self-martyrdom, and settled for a full face or three-quarter presentation.

They were not concerned with any impression they might make on others. Their experiments were purely for their private satisfaction.

Removed from the influence of Dargelos, thrown back upon himself by Elisabeth's withdrawal into silence, deprived of the stimulus of constant squabbling, Paul followed his own bent. Flabbiness set in; a tendency to sag. He started to go soft. She had guessed right. Nothing escaped her; she pounced on every symptom. Loathing everything that smacked of petty indulgences, lip-lickings, fireside cosiness, herself all fire and ice, she could not tolerate a luke-warm diet. As in the epistle to the angel of Laodicea: *She spewed it forth from her mouth*. Thoroughbred she was, and Paul too must be a thoroughbred.

On rushed the train, its human freight asleep beneath a flying tent of vapours rent intermittently by piercing screams; but on this first real journey of her life, deaf to the beat beat of the turning wheels, to the demented shrieking of the engine, blind to the smoke's wild mane that flew above them, she sat, this girl, intent upon her brother, searching his face with avid eyes.

A DISAPPOINTMENT WAS IN store for the young people. They arrived to find all hotels crammed to capacity. Apart from the room reserved for Gérard's uncle, there remained but one, at the far end of the corridor. It was suggested that the boys should share it, and that Elisabeth should have a camp bed in the adjoining bathroom. What in fact happened was that Elisabeth and Paul took possession of the bedroom, leaving the bathroom to Gérard.

By nightfall, the situation had deteriorated; Elisabeth wanted a bath and so did Paul. They sulked, raged, turned on one another, flung doors open, slammed them again at random, and ended finally at opposite ends of the same boiling bath, with Paul in fits of laughter. The sight of his seaweed limbs afloat in steam exasperated Elisabeth. An exchange of kicks ensued. Next day, at table, they were still kicking one another. Above the tablecloth their host saw smiling faces; a silent war went on below.

This subliminal struggle was not the only means by which, unconsciously, they managed to attract attention. The charm was working. Their table was rapidly becoming the focal point of a delighted curiosity. The get-together spirit was, to Elisabeth, anathema. She scorned "the others", or else fell madly in love with some total stranger. Hitherto the objects of her passion had been selected from the ranks of those matinée idols and Hollywood film stars whose garish outsize masks adorned her walls. The hotel afforded her no scope. The family parties were one and all hideous, gluttonous, and squalid. Their audience consisted of skinny little girls impervious to parental raps, craning their necks from afar to watch the marvellous table, the battle of limbs below, the peaceful countenances above.

For Elisabeth beauty was nothing but a pretext for ointments, clothes-pegs, distortions, secret masquerades in a scarecrow assortment of bits and pieces. Far from being a heady draught, her present success was merely a new kind of game, a change from the rigours of the Game of yore; she was a white-collar worker on a fishing expedition. They were both on holiday from the Room, from what they called the "convict settlement", for thus it had come to seem in their imaginations; a prison cell in which they were condemned to live, dragging one heavy chain between them, that prison's fascination unremembered, its poetic atmosphere (to Mariette so much more precious than to them) depreciated, the Game their only solace and release.

This new Game started in the dining-room. Elisabeth and Paul went at it, much to Gérard's horror, under his uncle's very nose; but the good man saw nothing but the features of twin seraphs.

The point of the Game was to scare the skinny little girls by sudden facial convulsions. They would wait patiently for the auspicious moment, a moment of general slackening of attention. Then was the moment to catch some tiny tot or other dislocated in her chair and gaping at the table, to transfix her first with a smile, then with a hideous grimace. She would look away in some alarm. They would repeat the treatment until, utterly unnerved, she burst into tears and complained to her mother. The mother then looked towards the table. Elisabeth beamed, the mother beamed responsively, the victim was slapped, scolded, and reduced to silence. The conspirators kept the score by nudging one another. The nudges provoked suppressed attacks of giggles, which included Gérard and finally exploded in the bedroom.

One evening, as they were about to leave the table, a diminutive child who had been chewing her way imperturbably through a dozen hideous faces, counterattacked by surreptitiously sticking out her tongue. They were delighted with her; she had actually given the Game a new dimension. They re-enacted their exploits as obsessively as any hunting-and-shooting addict, praising the child, discussing the day's play, deciding to tighten up the rules. Their verbal duels took on a fresh, more sanguinary lease of life.

Gérard implored them to go slow, to refrain from leaving the taps turned on, from trying to breathe under water, from chasing one another and brandishing chairs and emitting cries for help. Laughter and blows merged inextricably; for however conditioned an onlooker might be to their emotional somersaults, no one could foresee the moment when these two sundered portions of a single being would cease from strife and become one again: a phenomenon

which Gérard both dreaded and desired — desiring it for the sake of his uncle and the neighbours, dreading it because it meant the common front of Paul and Elisabeth against him.

Presently the Game expanded, invading lounge, street, beach, and esplanade. Elisabeth dragged Gérard in their wake. Crouching, clambering, scuttling, diabolically grinning and grimacing, the gang advanced in all directions. Panic spread. Wry-necked children, agape, with bulging eyes, were towed along by parents; slapped, spanked, incarcerated in their rooms, deprived of outings. Just when the scourge was at its peak, it ceased. The gang had discovered a more diverting occupation: stealing.

After them reeled Gérard, by this time too unnerved even to formulate his secret terrors. It was stealing not for profit, not out of craving for forbidden fruit: simply for stealing's sake. Mortal terror was the lure. They accompanied Gérard's uncle on shopping expeditions, returned with their pockets stuffed full of useless junk. The rules prohibited the theft of useful objects. One day, Elisabeth and Paul tried to make Gérard return a book because it was in French. He won conditional reprieve by agreeing to steal something extremely difficult. "A watering-can, for instance," declared Elisabeth.

They dressed him for the occasion in a gigantic cape; and thus accoutred, with a heart of lead, the luckless youth performed his task. What with his clumsiness, and the curious excrescence on his person of the watering-can, he made a profound impression on the ironmonger, who stood gazing after the retreating trio in a trance of arrested suspicion and of disbelief. "Hurry! Hurry! Idiot!"

whispered Elisabeth, "they're watching us." Once round the corner, out of danger, they breathed again and took to their heels.

A crab appeared in Gérard's dreams; its pincers had him by the shoulder. It was the ironmonger. He was calling the police. They had come to arrest him. He would be cut out of his uncle's will, etc. . . .

The loot — curtain-rings, screwdrivers, electric switches, labels, outsize gym shoes — went on piling up at the hotel into a sort of imitation treasure, as it were those sham pearls that women wear on holiday, leaving their real pearls at home.

As far as Elisabeth was concerned, this behaviour, as irresponsible as that of untrained children, naïvely cheeky to the point of crime, this inability to distinguish good from evil, this playing at pirates, stemmed from her instinct to save Paul from the flabbiness she dreaded in him. As long as she could keep him harried, scared stiff, grimacing, cursing, tearing up and down, he could not sink into inertia. We shall see where intuition led her before she had done with him and his re-education.

Then they came home. The ozone they had so casually inhaled had so signally restored them, mind and body, that Mariette found them changed almost beyond recognition. The brooch they brought her as a present was not a stolen object.

IT WAS THEN THAT the Room, like a great ship, put out to sea. Higher the waves, wider the horizons, rarer, more perilous, the cargo.

In their strange world of childhood, of action in inaction, as in the waking dream of opium eaters, to stay becalmed could be as dangerous as to advance at breakneck speed.

Gérard remained with them whenever his uncle went away on business. They dossed him down on a heap of cushions and covered him with old coats. Opposite him towered the theatre of their two beds. Each night, it was the lighting system that set the play in motion. The electric bulb happened to be over Paul's bed. Each night he covered it with a piece of bunting, and plunged the Room in reddish shadow. Each night Elisabeth objected to this partial black-out, jumped out of bed in a fury and removed the bunting. Paul put it back. Then ensued a tug-of-war which ended regularly with Paul triumphant, Elisabeth crushed, the bunting once more hoisted on the lamp. For since their return he had had the upper hand.

What she had feared when she had first seen him rise from his bed of sickness, half a head taller than herself, had come to pass: he was no longer content to play the invalid. Her recent efforts to promote his moral welfare were paying dividends far beyond her calculations. In vain she mocked him, saying: "Isn't it delicious? Remember, Giraffe – *everything's* delicious now. Films are *delicious*, books are *delicious*, what a *delicious* armchair, ginger pop and raspberry sodas are simply *delicious*. I say, Giraffe, isn't he revolting? Look at him! Look! Preening himself like a peacock!" It was no use, she knew her nursling was a child no longer. He had outstripped her in the race by almost a clear length. The very Room proclaimed it, seeming now to be constructed on two different levels. He was on the top floor, with all his magic properties within effortless reach; but she was consigned to the basement, obliged to dive or grovel ignominiously when she wanted to find hers.

But presently she hit on new ways of getting even with him. Laying down the weapons of a tomboy, she started to exploit her untried feminine resources, with Gérard for her stooge. She felt she could torment Paul more effectively before an audience: since Gérard came in handy for this purpose, she welcomed and made much of him.

The curtain rose at eleven o'clock at night. There were no matinées except on Sundays.

At seventeen, Elisabeth looked her age, no more, no less; Paul, on the other band, looked four years older than his fifteen years. He was beginning to be seen around the town, to frequent *delicious* cinemas and music-halls, to pick up *delicious* girls. To be solicited by a real tart was the most *delicious* thing of all.

[53]

When he came back he would recount his exploits. He described them with a candour well-nigh insensate, primitive; with a frankness so patently devoid of cynicism or vice that it seemed innocence itself. Elisabeth would tease, cross-question him, then suddenly, unpredictably, take exception to some comparatively harmless detail, and forthwith bridle, grab a paper, and retire behind it with a great show of icy concentration.

Gérard and Paul were wont to meet between eleven o'clock and midnight in one of the big Montmartre cafés, before coming home together. Meanwhile Elisabeth would stalk up and down the corridor in a frenzy of impatience.

At the sound of the hollow clang of the front door, she would quit her post and scurry back to the Room, to be discovered sitting with a hair net on her head, sticking her tongue out slightly, polishing her nails.

Paul flung his clothes off, Gérard put on his dressing-gown and was assisted into bed. The genius of the Room knocked thrice. The play began. But not one of the protagonists, it must be remembered, not even he who played the sole spectator, was consciously concerned with make-believe. In their archaic unawareness their play became the legend of eternal youth. Without their knowing it, the play — the Room — swung on the edge of myth.

The strip of bunting cast a ruddy glow upon the set. Naked, Paul wandered up and down, making his bed, smoothing the sheets, plumping the nest of pillows, setting out his stock-in-trade beside him on a chair. Propped on her left elbow, wearing the stern mask of a Byzantine empress, Elisabeth lay staring at her brother. With her right hand, she scratched her head. Having scratched it raw, she rubbed in ointment from a pot kept for this purpose by the pillow.

"Idiot!" declared Paul, adding: "If ever there was a sickening sight, it's that idiot and her grease-pot. She thinks it's good for the scalp. It's a tip she got from some Hollywood film mag. . . . Gérard!"

"What?"

"Are you listening?"

"Yes."

"Gérard, you're a jolly sight too patient. Go to sleep, don't let him be a nuisance."

Silence ensued. Paul bit his lips; his eye flashed fire. Wide, dewy, sublime, her gaze enfolded him, until at last he got into bed, tucked himself up, tried out a pose or two against the pillows – not seldom rejecting the whole arrangement and starting again from scratch until he had it absolutely to his liking.

The ideal state at last achieved, no power could have dislodged him from it. It was less a preparation for sleep than an embalming; in funeral bands, his food and drink and sacred *bric-à-brac* beside him, he set forth on his journey to the shades.

Night after night Elisabeth awaited this supreme moment of departure; through four long years, her cue had never altered. Incredible as it might seem, apart from a few trifling variations, the essence of the play had been preserved. It may be that elemental beings such as these follow some law of nature as mysteriously imperative as the law of flowers that close their petals up at night.

It was Elisabeth who introduced the variations. She thought up any number of surprises. One night, omitting the ritual of the ointment, she dived under the bed and produced a cut-glass salad bowl full of crayfish. Hugging it to her chest with both beautiful bare arms, she gloatingly surveyed the contents, then her brother.

"Gérard, have a crayfish? You simply must, this dressing's perfect." She knew Paul's passion for dressed crayfish sandwiches. Not daring to refuse, Gérard got out of bed.

"The cow!" muttered Paul. "She loathes crayfish. She loathes anything peppery. It's as much as she can do to get it down."

The act went on until the moment came when Paul could stand it no longer and begged her for a taste. Now she had him at her mercy, now his revolting greed could be chastised.

"Gérard, fancy a boy of sixteen abjectly begging for a crayfish! Could anything be lower? Honestly, you know, he'd lick them off the mat, he'd grovel for them. No, don't you take it to him; let him come and fetch it! The great sissy, he's simply too revolting — he's dying of greed but he can't be bothered to budge. He shan't have a crayfish. I'm too ashamed of him."

Then, if the spirit moved her, she would mount her tripod and give one of her famous impersonations of the Sibyl.

Paul would block his ears, or seize a book and start to read aloud, preferably from Saint-Simon or Charles Baudelaire. Deaf to the Oracle, he would say: "Listen, Gérard," and declaim:

> *J'aime son mauvais goût, sa jupe bigarrée,*
> *Son grand châle boiteux, sa parole égarée,*
> *Et son front rétréci.*

— little realizing how magically the stanza evoked the Room, the beauty of Elisabeth.

Meanwhile Elisabeth had seized a paper. In a voice intended as a parody of Paul's, she started to declaim the gossip column. The more Paul tried to shut her up, the louder rose her chant behind the screen of newspaper. But she was blind as well as barricaded.

Seizing his opportunity, Paul shot an arm out; before Gérard could stop him, he hurled a glass of milk at her.

"The wretch! The beast!"

Rage choked her. The soaking paper stuck to her like an adhesive plaster; the milk streamed over her in rivulets. But Paul should not have the satisfaction of reducing her to tears.

"Here a minute, Gérard," she went on. "Give me a hand, get a cloth, help me mop it up, chuck this paper in the kitchen." Then, lowering her voice: "And I was just going to let him have some crayfish . . . Want one? Look out, the milk's still dripping. Where's the cloth? I'm much obliged."

The burden of the crayfish came muffled to Paul's ears. Sleep was stealing over him. Crayfish had become a matter of indifference. Already he had weighed anchor. He had slipped the cable, cast overboard the ballast of his waking appetites; bound hand and foot, was launched upon the Stygian tide.

Now for the climax, the crucial situation she had laboured to manoeuvre into being, with the sole purpose of disrupting it. Once sure of having worn him down beyond recovery, she got up, came over to his bedside, and placed the salad bowl upon his knees.

"Go on, Horror. I'm not as mean as all that. You're welcome to your crayfish."

Alack for him, his head lay heavy on the tide of sleep, his swollen eyelids were fast sealed, his lips were drawing breath now in another air than man's.

"Go on, eat up. You said you wanted it, and now you don't. Now's your last chance, I'm off."

Then, like a severed head making a supreme last effort at communication, Paul opened his mouth a fraction.

"Well, if this doesn't take the cake! Hi! Paul! Here's your precious crayfish." She peeled one, inserted it between his jaws.

"He's chewing in his sleep! Do look, Gérard. It's most peculiar. The greedy pig! He really is the limit."

Her nostrils dilated, the tip of her tongue protruding, as if engrossed in scientific experiment, she went on feeding him. Intent, preoccupied, and mad she looked — a madwoman hunched over a dead child and cramming it with food.

Of this instructive session, Gérard retained one imprint and no more: namely, the moment when Elisabeth had addressed him for the first time by the familiar "tu".

Next morning, in mortal fear of getting his face slapped, he brought himself to make the self-same overture; feeling a pang of strangely sweet disturbance to find it tacitly accepted.

[58]

THE ROOM PROLONGED ITS rites into the small hours. This made for late awakenings. At eleven o'clock Mariette brought in the morning coffee. They left it untouched and went to sleep again. Next time she called them, cold coffee seemed an uninviting prospect. The third time, they were past getting up. The coffee, skin and all, was finally rejected, and Mariette bidden to pop downstairs to the newly-opened Café Charles and bring back drinks and sandwiches.

She would have preferred to practise the arts of a good Breton cook, but she had learned to subordinate her habits and wishes to their whims.

Occasionally, however, she got after them, chivvied them into the dining-room, and forced them to sit down to a square meal.

Elisabeth would slip a coat on over her nightdress and sink down in a dream, one elbow on the table, her hand propping her cheek, in a pose reminiscent of some allegorical female figure, symbolizing Science, or Agriculture, or the Seasons. Paul lolled beside her, sketchily attired. They ate silently, like strolling players taking a rest between performances. The empty hours of daylight weighed on them. They felt the tug of the current carrying them towards night, towards renewal, life, the Room.

Mariette was adept at keeping a room clean without disturbing its essential chaos. From four o'clock until five, she sewed. Lastly, having left them a cold supper, she went home. This was Paul's hour for roaming the deserted streets, for pursuing any girl whose form or features might suggest her prototype in Baudelaire's sonnet.

Alone at home, Elisabeth went on leaning, standing, sitting in disdainful attitudes. She never left the house except to buy surprises, hurrying home to hide them. She wandered uneasily from room to room, sick with the horror of one room, one room where lay a body: an anonymous dead woman, not the mother she remembered and who still lived on within her.

At fall of night, her restlessness increasing, she advanced into the dead centre of the Room and stood at attention, her arms along her sides, staring ahead of her through the engulfing shadows. The Room was sinking, about to be submerged; and she too was sinking, motherless. She stood like a captain on the bridge, and let herself go down.

B EYOND THE BOUNDARIES OF the ordinary world of lives and houses, unguessed, undreamed of in their commonsense philosophy, lies the vast realm of the improbable: a world too disordered, so it would seem, to hold together for a fortnight, let alone for several years. And yet these lives, these houses continue to maintain a precarious equilibrium in defiance of all laws of man and nature. All the same, persons who base their calculations on the inexorable pressure of the force of circumstance assume, correctly, that such lives are doomed.

The world owes its enchantment to these curious creatures and their fancies; but its multiple complicity rejects them. Thistledown spirits, tragic, heartrending in their evanescence, they must go blowing headlong to perdition. And yet, all started harmlessly, in childish games and laughter . . .

Thus in the rue Montmartre, three years, monotonous and unremittingly intense, passed by. Elisabeth and Paul, incapable of growing up, went on rocking their twin cradles. Gérard loved Elisabeth.

Elisabeth and Paul adored, devoured each other. Regularly once a fortnight, after some nocturnal quarrel, Elisabeth packed a bag and was off to live in a hotel.

Night after stormy night, followed by heavy-lidded mornings; then the long afternoons on which they drifted, drowsy, blind as moles. Sometimes Elisabeth took Gérard for her escort, while Paul was hunting on his own; but nothing that they saw or heard belonged to them as individuals. They were inexorably compelled to carryback the sweets they rifled, to feed the common store of honey.

They had no inkling, this orphaned penniless pair, that they were outlaws, living on borrowed time, beyond the battle, on fate's capricious bounty. It seemed to them no more than natural that Gérard's uncle and the doctor should continue to provide for them.

Wealth is an inborn attitude of mind, like poverty. The pauper who has made his pile may flaunt his spoils, but cannot wear them plausibly. These children had been born so rich that nothing in the way of worldly riches could possibly have changed their lives. Had they inherited a fortune overnight, they would have been immune from it.

Indolent, frivolous, they were the living refutation of the Puritan ideal, the living exemplar of these words of the philosopher: *vital essences, volatile, indifferent, drinkers at the sacred fount.*

They had as little instinct for planning, study, job-hunting, wire-pulling, as a pampered lapdog has for guarding sheep. In the newspapers, they read the crime reports and nothing else.

Uncontainable in any social framework, they were of that tribe that New York reforms at home and banishes for choice to Paris.

When, therefore, to the consternation of Paul and Gérard, Elisabeth suddenly announced her intention of looking for a job, she was in no way moved by practical considerations. She was sick, she declared, of being a slavey. Paul could jolly well look after himself. In any case, she was nineteen, her health was going to pieces, she would not stand it a day longer.

"You see, Gérard," she declared, "Paul's got no ties, and besides, he's useless, he's no good, he's a half-wit, practically mad. I'll have to fend for myself. Besides, what's to become of him if I don't work? I must earn my living. I shall get a job. I must."

Gérard understood. It had just dawned on him that the stern opening bars of a new theme were sounding in the Room. All ready to be gone, Paul lay embalmed, the passive victim of this unfamiliar onslaught.

"Poor kid," she went on, "he does need help. You see, he's really not much better. The doctor . . . (no, it's all right, Giraffe, he's asleep), the doctor's awfully worried about him. He'll never be able to go back to school again. It's not his fault, I'm not blaming him, it's just that I've got a chronic invalid on my hands. To think that one snowball, one little snowball, could do him in like this."

"Devil! Devil!" thought Paul. He went on feigning sleep; but a nervous twitch betrayed his agitation.

Solicitously, finger on lip, Elisabeth bent over him, then presently began again, turning the screws with expert fingers, stressing the pathos of his present state. When Gérard protested, pointing out

[63]

how well he looked, how much he had grown, how strong he was, she countered with his greed, his spinelessness, his slackness.

Finally, unable to contain himself a moment longer, he stirred, as if beginning to wake up. At once she changed the subject, in honeyed accents asked him what he wanted.

Paul was now seventeen years old. This many a month he could have passed for twenty. He had outgrown sugar, outgrown crayfish. It was time, his sister thought, to raise the stakes.

Sleep having placed him at a disadvantage, a change of tactics seemed to Paul advisable. He made a sudden charge. At once she switched from plaintiveness to rank abuse. He was a worm, a downright spiv. He'd be the death of her. She wouldn't put it past him to set up as a pimp and let her walk the streets.

She for her part was nothing but a windbag, a figure of fun, a useless fatuous old donkey.

These epithets compelled her to abandon speech for action. She besought Gérard to introduce her to a woman of his acquaintance, head of one of the great fashion houses. She would be a salesgirl.

GÉRARD INTRODUCED HER TO the dressmaker, who was staggered by her beauty. Unfortunately, however, all salesgirls must know foreign languages. She could only be engaged as a mannequin. She would be in good hands: there happened to be another orphan, Agatha, in their employ; Agatha would keep an eye on her.

Salesgirl? Mannequin? Between the two Elisabeth could see no difference in status. On the contrary, her début as a mannequin seemed to her tantamount to being launched, or almost, as an actress. The agreement was concluded, and had a further notable result. She had expected Paul to be upset; and in fact, for a number of obscure reasons, he did quite genuinely fall into transports of rage and indignation, waving his arms, shouting that he didn't fancy being the brother of a high-class tart, that he'd sooner see her on the streets.

"I'd rather not," retorted Elisabeth, "I might run into you."

"My poor girl," sneered Paul, "take a look at yourself in the glass.

[65]

You'll only make an exhibition of yourself. You'll be out on your fanny within an hour. Mannequin, indeed! Stick yourself up as a scarecrow. That's more your line."

To be a mannequin requires a harsh apprenticeship; the first day is as terrifying, as humiliating, as one's first day at school. Emerging from a long dark tunnel, Elisabeth stepped up on to the dais, under the glaring arc-lamps. Convinced that she was hideous, fearing the worst, she flamed among the other sophisticated, jaded models in all her untamed alien beauty. Enviously they stared, started to whisper among themselves; but something about her gave her immunity from open persecution, and they decided to ignore her. She found her isolation a sore trial. She watched the others and tried to copy their way of bearing down on a prospective client, as if about to demand a public apology, then at the last moment turning disdainfully away. But she was not the fashionable type. She was depressed by the boring frocks they made her model. She became Agatha's stand-in.

A warm affection – for Elisabeth a hitherto unknown emotion – grew up gradually between the two motherless girls, uniting them in a friendship that was to prove fatal to them both. They were both social misfits. Whatever moments they could snatch from modelling they spent together, curled up in their white overalls on divans strewn with model furs, exchanging books and confidences, and generally acting as a mutual tonic.

So all the wheels began to turn; the parts to be assembled began to travel, with smooth coordination, stage after stage, to their appointed ends: a moment more, and Agatha was in the Room.

Elisabeth had half hoped that Paul would register some protest. She had warned him that the girl had a silly name. But on the contrary, Paul said, the name Agatha was illustrious: it had been immortalized in one of the most beautiful poems in the French language.

THE PROCESS BY WHICH Gérard had been drawn, through Paul, towards Elisabeth was now operating, less deviously, in the case of Agatha, and drawing her, through Elisabeth, to Paul. Paul found the presence of Agatha disturbing. Unpractised in the art of self-analysis, he classified her as *delicious*, and left it at that.

In fact, what he had done was to bestow upon Agatha the vague prolific fantasies which had silted over Dargelos. This struck him with the blinding force of a revelation, one evening when the two girls were in the Room. The treasure was on view, and Elisabeth explaining it, when Agatha seized the photograph of Dargelos dressed as Athalie and cried:

"Have you got my photograph?" in a voice so strange that Paul lifted his head from his sarcophagus and stayed reclining on his elbows in the pose of *Les jeunes Chrétiens d'Antinoé*.

"It's not your photograph," replied Elisabeth.

"No, I see it isn't, the clothes are different. But it's incredible, the likeness to an old one of me. I'll bring it. It's exactly the same — me, me! — the living image. Who is it?"

"It's not a girl, duck. It's that chap I told you about, the one at

Paul's school who threw the snowball . . . You're perfectly right, he is like you. Paul, *is* he like Agatha to look at?"

At these words, the likeness which, till now, he had managed to suppress, burst ineluctably across the threshold. Gérard recognized the fatal profile. Agatha turned towards Paul, holding up a rectangle of white; and it was Dargelos Paul saw against the shadows, brandishing the snowball, about to strike him down.

He let his head fall back and answered faintly: "No, my love, no. The photograph has got a look of you, but you're not really like him in the least."

This patent lie made Gérard anxious. The resemblance absolutely hit one in the face.

In truth, there were buried levels of his spirit which Paul preferred to leave untouched. The mine was rich and deep, loaded with unimaginable treasure: he was afraid of his own clumsiness. *Delicious* was not a term applicable to anything below the crust of that volcano, whose heady vapours numbed his ravished senses.

From that night on, the loom of Paul-and-Agatha began to weave a criss-cross pattern. The wheel of fortune had come round full circle, pride had had its downfall, proud Dargelos of the marble heart, insensible to love, had suffered metamorphosis, was now a shy young girl whom Paul could wholly subjugate.

Elisabeth thrust the photograph back in the drawer. Next morning she found it on the mantelpiece. She frowned. She made no comment, but her thoughts raced ahead. In a flash she realized that all Paul's pinups – glamour girls, gunmen, sleuths and all – were prototypes of Agatha and Dargelos-Athalie.

A nameless consternation strangled her. "It's the limit," she told herself, "he's double-crossing me. He's cheating." She decided to pay him back in his own coin, to play up Agatha at Paul's expense while feigning to ignore their goings-on.

The aura of family likeness in the Room was an indubitable fact; although, had it been pointed out to Paul, he would have been astonished. His pursuit of one physical type was quite unconscious. And yet his fascination with it and the fascination he himself unwittingly exerted on his sister drove two straight lines through the disorder of their lives, lines destined to meet as inexorably as in a theorem by Euclid; like those two lines which, starting inimically at the base, converging, form the apex of the classic Grecian pediment.

Agatha and Gérard had established their right to co-tenancy of this unlikely Room, or rather of this gipsy camp; for that was what it was gradually coming to resemble. The horse was lacking, but not the ragged children. Elisabeth suggested that Agatha should come to live with them. Mariette could get the spare room ready — "Mummy's room", the room of standing alone, of remembering, of waiting to be swallowed up in darkness. But Agatha had no such melancholy associations with it; a thorough cleansing and a lamp or two would make of it a pleasant bedroom.

Gérard helped Agatha to bring along some suitcases. The domestic habits, the wakings and the sleepings, the quarrels, the storms, the calms, the café and its sandwiches, were hers already.

Every evening, when they had finished work, the girls found Gérard waiting, either to take them for a stroll or see them home.

Mariette prepared the same cold supper; they took it off the table and made a picnic of it; next morning Mariette came back and swept the eggshells up.

Paul was determined to make the most of this propitious turn of Fortune's wheel. He had no coat-of-mail arrogance, like Dargelos, to buckle on; but other well-tried weapons lay ready to his hand: in other words, the gentle Agatha became his butt. When Elisabeth flew to her defence he turned the tables on them, sided with Agatha in order to upset his sister. This paid off nicely for all four of them: for Elisabeth, thus enabled to enlarge the scope of her activities; for Gérard, given a moment's welcome respite; for Agatha, spell-bound by Paul's insolence; and finally for Paul himself. He was no Dargelos; but insolence has a glamour all its own; and with Agatha's cooperation, and Elisabeth for target, he found he could exploit it.

Agatha embraced her role with sacrificial ardour, feeling that the Room contained a force of love so potent that though it must intermittently explode, it could not damage her. It set her tingling violently as from electric shock, violent, yet it was positive in its effect, life-giving as the salt wind blowing from the sea.

Her parents, drug-addicts, had maltreated her, and ended by putting their heads in a gas oven. She had been rescued by the manager of an important fashion house, who happened to live in the same block of flats. He introduced her to the head of his firm, who took her on as an apprentice and subsequently as a mannequin. Acquainted as she was with the clenched fist, with malice, and abuse, she recognized these portents in the Room, but with a difference. Here they evoked the battering wave, the stinging wind, the bolt that falls at random and in pure wantonness may strip the shepherd.

The contrast was a basic one, but all the same her experience of drug-addicts had conditioned her to the seamy side of life, to threatening voices, footsteps, broken furniture, cold snacks in the middle of the night. Behaviour normally calculated to raise a maiden blush failed to dismay her. The harsh school from which she had emerged had left its mark on her. Something savage lurked around her eyes and nostrils, recalling Dargelos at first sight, his mask of scorn.

She had ascended into the Room as if into the heaven of her hell. She could live at last, she could draw breath. Nothing worried her; she had no fear that her new friends might take to drugs; their addiction was, she knew, a natural and self-engendered one, and any external stimulus would have been redundant.

But now and then a kind of delirium seemed to take possession of them. The Room waxed feverish with images reflected in distorting mirrors. Then a dark shadow fell across her; she would ask herself if this mysterious elixir they imbibed was none the less as noxious, habit-forming, as likely as any other drug to lead to the gas oven. Then some shift of ballast, some steadying of the keel would come to reassure her and dispel her doubts.

But she had divined the truth, the workings in them of the wonderous substance. The drug was in their bloodstream.

The cycles of drug-addiction proceed by gradual stages, each period producing its characteristic phenomena and transformations. The frontiers are not marked; but along each one of them stretches a no-man's land of havoc and disturbance. The area of vision breaks up kaleidoscopically, to form fresh patterns.

Less and less did the Game predominate in Elisabeth's new life, and even in that of Paul. As for Gérard, he was completely absorbed in Elisabeth and had given it up. Every attempt made by Paul and Elisabeth to resuscitate it ended dismally, and merely made them irritable. They could no longer *be gone*. The dream wavered, its thread thinned out, dissolved. The truth was, they were gone elsewhere. Past masters in escaping from themselves, they accepted the new force which drove them inwards, but took it for distraction. Where formerly they had swung airily above the tragic stage, like gods and goddesses on wires at a command performance, they were now immersed in the dramatic plot itself. Their own performances left much to be desired. To look within requires self-discipline, and this they lacked. Primeval darkness, ghosts of feeling, were all that they encountered. "Damn! Damn!" cried Paul, exasperated. They all looked up. "Damn!" meant that, to his furious annoyance, some floating wraith of Agatha had cut across his preparations for departure to the land of shades: the cause of the disaster was too plain for Paul, self-engrossed, or for his sister, watching him, to recognize it. He insisted that the fault was Agatha's and made her bear the brunt of his ill-temper. As for Elisabeth, who was also endeavouring to put out to sea, only to founder on hitherto uncharted reefs, she snatched the opportunity to turn her observation outwards. She misinterpreted Paul's spitefulness, thinking: "He's fed up with Agatha because she reminds him of Dargelos," and failing to discern the passion that provoked it. Thus once again, between these two antagonists – as inexpert in self-analysis as they had once been learned in the lore of the unknowable – the bitter duel was on, with Agatha for gauge.

But brawling leads to laryngitis. The wordy battles petered out, then ceased, and once again the warriors found harsh reality imping-ing on their dream, disturbing childhood's vegetative existence and scattering all its harmless toys.

What cryptic impulse of self-preservation, what psychic nerve had momentarily stayed Elisabeth's hand, that day of adding Dargelos to the treasure? No doubt her senses had vibrated to the complex instincts Paul was trying to suppress, to the self-conscious, unconvincing tone of voice he had assumed to ask her: "Shall we keep it?" Be that as it may, this much was certain: the photograph of Dargelos was no idle toy. Its suggestion had been flung out with the jaunty disingenuousness of one caught red-handed. She had complied with patent lack of zest, and left the room with knowing and ironic shrugs at Paul and Gérard, just to be on the safe side, just to keep them guessing – just to impress on them that whatever their little game might be, she was already on to it.

Stealthily, insidiously, it would appear, the silence of the drawer had wrought upon the picture, to bring about the sinister merging of two separate images. That Agatha, holding up the photograph, had brandished not Dargelos but his snowball, was scarcely a matter for surprise.

PART TWO

FOR SEVERAL DAYS THE Room had been running into heavy weather. Elisabeth had persistently tormented Paul by enigmatic looks and cryptic references to a "*delicious* something", which he would not be allowed to share. She treated Agatha as her confidante, Gérard as her accomplice; and countered any direct approach to the forbidden subject with a great display of winks. These machinations succeeded beyond her wildest hopes. Paul writhed and twisted on the rack of curiosity, pride alone preventing him from trying to pump Agatha or Gérard, who, under pain of terrible reprisals, were sworn to silence. At length curiosity prevailed. Posting himself at what Elisabeth had nicknamed the "stage door", he spied on the conspirators and discovered that not only Gérard but a dashing young man in a sports car was waiting for them.

The scene that occurred that night was cataclysmic. The girls were prostitutes, foul prostitutes, and Gérard was a pimp. He himself would leave the house. Then they could use it as a brothel. It was only to be expected. All mannequins were tarts, low ones at that.

His sister was a bitch on heat, she had corrupted Agatha, and Gérard was behind it all.

Agatha wept. Gérard lost his temper, and in spite of Elisabeth's mild and repeated interjections of: "Leave him alone, Gérard, he's absurd," insisted on explaining that the young man was a friend of his uncle's, was called Michael, was an American Jew, was enormously rich; and that in any case they had been on the point of coming clean and introducing him to Paul.

Never, shrieked Paul, would he consent to meet the "filthy Jew": he was coming along tomorrow at the appointed hour to slap his face.

"It's too squalid," he concluded, his eyes glittering. "You take an inexperienced young girl along with you simply to sell her to a Jew. I suppose you're hoping for a rake-off."

"Rubbish, my dear fellow," retorted Elizabeth. "You're barking up the wrong tree, I do assure you. I'm the one Michael's got his eye on. He wants to marry me, and what's more I like him very much."

"Marry you? Marry you? You must be mad. Have you looked in the glass lately? Don't you realize you're a monster? Do you really think anyone would want to marry you, you prize idiot? He must be pulling your leg."

And he burst into hysterical laughter.

Elisabeth was well aware that it was a matter of complete indifference to Paul, as to herself, whether people were or were not Jewish. She felt suffused with warmth and well-being. Her heart so overflowed it could have cracked the walls. How she revelled in this pseudo-laughter! How grim his jaw looked now! What sport indeed to goad him to such frenzy!

Next morning, Paul felt that he had made a fool of himself. His outburst, he secretly admitted, had been unnecessarily extravagant. Quite forgetting that he had suspected the American of designs on Agatha, he now told himself that Elisabeth was her own mistress, that he couldn't care less whom she chose to marry. He wondered why on earth he had flown off the handle.

After a period of sulks, he finally let himself be persuaded to meet Michael.

Michael was in every way the Room's antithesis. This was so evident that no attempt was ever made to introduce him to it. He personified the outside world. One saw at a glance that he was of the world worldly, that his whole treasure was laid up on earth, and as for ecstasy, his only chance of it would come when driving at a hundred miles an hour, at the wheel of the latest thing in high-powered sports cars.

His film-star personality captured Paul who promptly set aside his principles and fell for him. Drunk with speed, they went whirling through the countryside at all hours other than those tacitly consecrated by the four initiates to the ceremonies of the Room; and by Michael, in all simplicity, to sleep.

Their midnight mysteries took nothing from the stature of the absent Michael. He was invoked, worshipped, completely re-created.

How could he know, when next they met, that magic juices were laid upon their eyelids, making them madly dote upon him after the manner of Titania in *A Midsummer Night's Dream*?

"Why shouldn't I marry Michael?"

"Why shouldn't Elisabeth marry Michael?"

In the future their separate rooms would be assured. They lost their heads and sketched wild plans for rooms-to-be — domestic projects as ambitious and grotesque as those confided to reporters by the celebrated Siamese twins.

Gérard alone lacked stomach for the game. He silently withdrew. Never would he have aspired to marry the Pythoness, the Sacred Virgin. It took a melodramatic film type, an ignorant young racing driver, to desecrate the inner shrine and carry off its inmate.

And the Room went on, and the wedding preparations were afoot, and still the hair's-breadth balance was maintained: the clown's act, in the interval, the sickening ever-mounting pile of chairs, the clown ascending, step by giddy step.

Nausea, giddiness, satiety of spirit now, sharper to the palate than the old physical satiety of childhood's barley-sugar orgies — a glutton's diet of sensation, a cloying hotch-potch of misrule, disorder.

But Michael had no notion of these things. He would have been astonished to discover that he had picked a vestal virgin for his chosen bride. He was in love with a ravishing young girl and wished to marry her. Lightheartedly he brought her his splendid house in Paris, his cars, his fortune, and laid them at her feet.

For her own room Elisabeth settled on a Louis XVI period décor, leaving Michael as sole tenant of the reception rooms, the music room, gymnasium, and swimming pool, besides an absurd sort of Town Hall of a room, with windows level with the tree-tops,

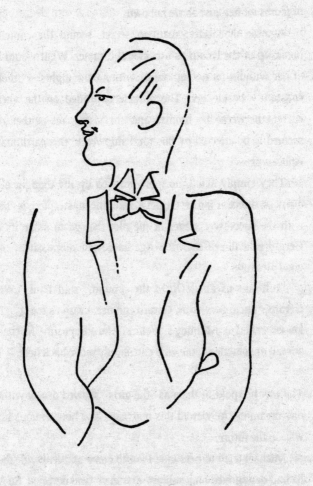

that did duty for dining-room, billiard-room, and fencing-gallery. Agatha was to live with them. Elisabeth had set aside a little suite of rooms for her, just above her own.

Agatha shed bitter tears in secret, seeing the contemplated break-up of the Room as a personal disaster. What would become of her without its potent magic, without the nights? Without Paul constantly beside her? The miracle depended on the alternating current between the brother and the sister. Yet neither of them seemed to be affected by this total shipwreck, this earthquake, this Apocalypse.

They simply acted, no more worried by the thought of consequences, direct or indirect, than a dramatic masterpiece is concerned with the successive stages of the plot that go to make its climax. Gérard was all self-sacrifice. Agatha bowed submissively to Paul's good pleasure.

"It'll suit us all down to the ground," said Paul. "Whenever Gérard's uncle goes away, Gérard can use Agatha's room." (They no longer called it Mummy's room.) "And supposing Michael went abroad or something, the girls can simply move back here."

The way he spoke of them as "the girls" showed clearly with what a day-dream eye he viewed this marriage, and how tenuous his grasp was on the future.

Michael tried to persuade Paul to come and live with them, but he had determined on a solitary existence, and declined. So Michael undertook entire financial responsibility for the rue Montmartre household, with Mariette for steward.

The wedding ceremony was brief, witnessed by a couple of the trustees appointed to administer the bridegroom's unimaginable fortune. No sooner was it over than Michael, thinking to give Elisabeth and Agatha a chance to settle in, jumped into his racing car *en route* for a week in Eze, to see the architect who was building him a villa. Domestic life would start when he came back.

But the genius of the Room was vigilant.

Need it be told in words? On the road between Cannes and Nice, Michael met his death.

It was one of those cars with a low chassis. The wind caught his long scarf, wrapped it round the wheel, and in one savage second strangled him. The car skidded, buckled, reared against a tree, and was nothing, but a heap of wreckage with one wheel spinning like a roulette wheel . . . slower, slower, slower in the silence.

ELISABETH FELT QUITE INCAPABLE of coping with all the wearisome legal paraphernalia of her widowhood: all she was to know of marriage was a series of meetings with solicitors, documents to be signed, and widow's weeds. Though freed from financial responsibility, the doctor and Gérard's uncle now found their burden even heavier and more thankless than before. Elisabeth had no compunction in letting everything devolve on them.

They spent all their time with the executors, sorting papers and totting up columns of figures representing sums of incalculable magnitude.

Mention has been made already of the inherent richness of Elisabeth and Paul – a richness so entire, so absolute, that nothing in the way of further worldly wealth could possibly accrue to them. Now that they had inherited a fortune, this was self-evident. What did affect them was the dramatic impact of the accident. They had been fond of Michael. Now, by virtue of his strange nuptials and astounding death, this youth without a secret was translated into the most secret places. The scarf that sprang to stop his mortal breath had touched the door and flung him, dead, into the Room.

WITH AGATHA'S DEPARTURE, PAUL lost all relish for domestic solitude. The thought of living alone had made some sense in the old days, when he and his sister had wrestled over bags of sweets and squabbled greedily; not now, when the years had given him desires more difficult to compass.

He did not know precisely what it was he lacked; but the taste of solitude, once coveted, was ashes on his tongue. Persuaded by Elisabeth, he took advantage of this state of negativity to change his mind and set up house with her.

She gave him Michael's room, divided from her own by an enormous bathroom. The coloured staff of four, including the chef, gave notice and went back to America. Mariette replaced them by a woman from her native Brittany. The chauffeur stayed on.

No sooner was Paul settled in than they began to gravitate towards a dormitory.

Agatha felt frightened, all alone on the floor above . . . Paul couldn't sleep in his four-poster . . . Gérard's uncle had gone to Germany to inspect some factories . . . In no time, Agatha had moved downstairs to share Elisabeth's bed, while Paul dragged his

[85]

bedding over to the couch and made himself a burrow, and Gérard wrapped himself in a cocoon of shawls.

It was here, in this abstraction, this Room fortuitously assembled or dispersed, that Michael had come to dwell since the disaster. O, Sacred Virgin! . . . Gérard had guessed truly. Never would Elisabeth be his, Michael's, or any man's in the whole world. Love made him clairvoyant, and he beheld the impenetrable circle that severed her from human love, that none might violate, save at the price of life itself. And even could the virgin have been ravished by the living Michael, only by his death could he have won possession of the shrine.

THE READER WILL REMEMBER that one of the features of the mansion was a gallery, which more or less did duty for study, dining-room, and billiard-room. Architecturally considered, it was an anomalous design, for it served no conceivable purpose and led nowhere. A strip of stair-carpeting had been laid down over the linoleum from end to end of one side of the room. On the other side, beneath a cheap electric light fixture suspended from the ceiling, stood a dining-room table, a few chairs, and a number of plywood screens. The screens partitioned off the so-called dining-room from the so-called study, where a sofa, one or two leather armchairs, a revolving book case, and a globe were disposed haphazard round another table – an architect's trestle table – furnished with a reading lamp that cast the only focal beam of light in the whole room.

Beyond this, despite a rocking-chair or two, all seemed immensities of vacant space; then came the billiard-table, monumental in its isolation. Here and there, tall windows cast watchful slats of light upon the ceiling and bathed the décor in an unreal lunar radiance.

It seemed a stage, set for the sound of a casement cautiously pushed up, the muffled thud of a stealthy leap, the spark of a torch in darkness.

Silence and spectral sheen recalled the old rue Montmartre drawing-room frailly suspended in a cage of snow-light; and even tenuously suggested the snow-bound, shrunken aspect of the Cité Monthiers just before the battle. There was the same sense of isolation, of expectancy; and in the high windows a faint simulacrum of those pallid walls.

Altogether the Room seemed the result of one of those fantastic aberrations or miscalculations, comparable to the omission of kitchen or staircase, in the architect's original blueprint.

Michael had rebuilt the house; but the problem of reconciling this cul-de-sac, which seemed to lurk at the end of every turning, with the rest of the design had continued to defeat him. Such failures, however, were his human opportunity; they marked the point where mechanical efficiency yielded to life itself. Here, in this dead-end alley, in a scarcely breathing structure, before the immitigable onslaught of lifeless stone and metal, Life stood at bay. Here she had fled for sanctuary, crouching in this enormous niche like a banished and distraught princess outwitting her pursuers.

Locally, the house was not without admirers. "You can't call it ostentatious, anyway," they said. "Nothing flash about it. That's saying something, for a chap as rich as Croesus." As for his fellow-countrymen, who would have found nothing to impress them, they had as little inkling as poor Michael how American it was in essence.

Better than luxurious marble fittings and ornamental ironwork, it evoked New York — the New York of freak religions, theosophy,

Christian science, the Klu-Klux-Klan; of crazy endowments and eccentric heiresses, of morticians, spiritualist seances, the occult world of Edgar Allen Poe.

It suggested also some sort of waiting-room in a mental hospital; or the stage set for the materialization of departed spirits reporting their demise. The Room was not without a hint, besides, of the Jewish-baronial taste for the flamboyant — for that sort of gothic penthouse chapel, forty storeys up, whose lady inmates pace up and down the nave, burn wax tapers, and play upon the organ. For there is a greater demand for tapers in New York than in Lourdes, or Rome itself, or for that matter any holy city in the world.

This gallery designed for frightened children who, waking, listen to the creaking dark, who dare not traverse certain corridors, this monstrosity, this lumber room was Michael's sweetness, his vein of poetry, his Achilles' heel; betraying some quality endemic to his nature, something innate, not borrowed from the children, that was to make him worthy of them both. His fitness, had they known it, for election to the Room, his marriage and his tragic fate, were here prophetically made manifest. Here lay the answer to what had seemed so baffling: Elisabeth had chosen him, not for his fortune or his animal spirits or his well-cut suits; not even for his sex appeal; it was for his death that she had chosen him.

And it was in the nature of things that the children, in ransacking the whole house to find their Room again, should overlook the gallery. Back and forth between their rooms they drifted, like souls in torment.

No longer were their nights transparent, a light wraith vanishing at cockcrow, but an unquiet ghost, brooding above them. Having at last achieved their separate rooms, they were determined to hang on to them, and either shut themselves up and sulked, or went shuffling defiantly from one room to another, tight-lipped, with daggers in their eyes.

They knew, half-fearfully, that the gallery was singing to them in a siren voice. They stood on the threshold, hesitating, listening, taking stock.

One of the room's peculiar properties, and not the least attractive, was its likeness to a ship at anchor, moored by a single cable, swinging freely.

No sooner out of it than one found it quite impossible to locate; back one came, only to find that every other room had shifted its original position. The sole clue, and that a feeble one, was a faint sound of washing-up from the direction of the kitchen.

And all combined to weave a spell, to recall the drowsy magic of old childhood holidays in Swiss hotels when, drunk with the thrill of riding in the ski-lift, one lay relaxed, staring sheer down at the whole world, and at the glacier opposite — a palace made of crystal, so close, so close . . . (if you were to lean — to stretch your hand out, you could almost touch it).

The hour had struck for Michael to become their guide, to pick up the golden wand, to trace the boundaries, and lead them to the destined place.

ONE NIGHT, WHEN ELISABETH'S insistent attempts to prevent Paul from going to sleep had been as usual sulkily resisted, he suddenly jumped up, slammed the door, and made a dash for the gallery.

Deficient though he was by nature in powers of observation, he was intensely receptive to emanations, knowing by instinct how to assimilate them and turn them to his purpose.

No sooner folded in those tenebrous vistas, those alternating panels of light and darkness, no sooner trapped amid the litter of this derelict film set, than he became a cat, wary, his every sense alert. His eyes began to glitter. He went padding here and there, stopping, snuffing, not consciously aware of recognition, unable to elucidate the double images – the Cité Monthiers hidden in the Room, the floor of snow beneath this midnight silence – but feeling along his nerves the subterranean tremors of a buried life.

He sat down to inspect the study, got up again, dragged some screens over, set them up round his armchair to be his boat, lay down, put his feet up, and bent himself beatifically to the Game.

But the barque put out for the dim flood, and left him stranded.

He was perturbed. His pride was injured. His vengeance upon Dargelos in the guise of a young girl had been a hopeless flop. He was in thrall to Agatha. And instead of realizing that he loved her, that it was her gentle nature that subdued him, that he should surrender, he reared and plunged in a fierce struggle to shake off this incubus, for so he saw her, avert this evil doom.

To drain the contents of one barrel into another through a length of rubber tubing depends upon one simple operation – the turning of a tap.

Next day Paul started building himself a primitive sort of hut, without a roof, with screens for walls, and settled in. Both in its outer eccentricity and its inner chaos, this curious enclosure seemed integrally designed to suit the unearthly aspect of the Room. Paul brought along books, empty boxes, treasure, and plaster bust to furnish it. His dirty linen began piling up. The scene was reflected in an enormous mirror. The armchair was replaced by a camp bed. The piece of bunting bestrode the reading lamp.

Elisabeth, Agatha, and Gérard began by paying him formal calls; but presently, unable to resist the spell of this upholstered landscape, they migrated in a body on Paul's heels.

Life began again. They pitched camp. Moonbeams and shadows were their company.

By the end of a week, thermos flasks were doing duty for the Café Charles, and the screens had been extended to form a single room – a desert island in a sea of linoleum.

The sense of discomfort resulting from the separate rooms

had caused Paul and Elisabeth to give way to sour ill-humour. Agatha and Gérard attributed the change to the disturbed atmosphere caused by their alien presence. It made them feel unwanted; they drew closer and started going out together. A common ailment formed the immutable basis of their friendship. Agatha worshipped Paul, as Gérard worshipped Elisabeth. They dared not voice their love, and suffered it in silence. Lowly they stood before a double altar; Agatha before the youth snow-shrouded, Gérard before the Iron Maiden, lifting eyes of adoration.

Never would it have crossed their minds to aspire to more than a vague benevolence in return. They marvelled at the tolerance vouchsafed them, and fearing to presume upon it, or to fail in tact, assiduously withdrew from the charmed circle at every opportunity.

Elisabeth kept forgetting that she had several cars at her disposal. The chauffeur was obliged to jog her memory. One night, when she had gone out for a drive with Gérard and Agatha, leaving Paul locked in his self-chosen dungeon, he stumbled suddenly upon the truth: he was in love.

His head in a whirl, he had been staring at the photograph, that counterfeit of Agatha, when the discovery felled him like a thunderbolt. The scales dropped from his eyes. He was like one who, after prolonged poring over a monogram, suddenly sees letters stand out clearly in what had formerly seemed mere tracery devoid of meaning.

The screens were hung with all his old trophies from the rue Montmartre, after the manner of an actor's dressing-room. Instantly, like a Chinese swamp studded with lotus amorously exploding into flower at dawn, the screens unfolded all their many faces.

Emerging from multiplicity – here through a gangster's features, there through an actress's – the prototype took shape. First glimpsed in Dargelos, pursued through the murk and glimmer of the casual streets, focused on the brittle screens, it crystallized at last in Agatha. How many tentative designs, how many rough sketches for the face of love before the final portrait! He had imagined himself in thrall to an accidental likeness between a schoolboy and a girl; but now he knew with what deliberation Fate first picks her weapon, then lifts it, aims it, finds the heart.

And this time there had been no question of Paul's secret predilection for one certain type: fate and fate alone had selected Agatha out of the whole world of girls, to be Elisabeth's companion. Who knows? – it may have been in that grim kitchen, by the lethal gas stove, that the knot had first been tied.

Paul marvelled at the fact of their encounter; but his sudden clairvoyance was confined to one sole area, that of love. Otherwise a greater marvel might have felled him utterly: namely, Fate the lacemaker implacably at work, holding upon her knees the cushion of our lives, and stuffing it with pins.

Without one solid plank beneath his feet, adrift within his room, Paul dreamed of love. For a time Agatha remained an abstract figure, disembodied, he, isolated in his ecstasy. Looking in the glass, he saw with a shock that all the tension had faded from his face; and was ashamed of his past folly and its mask of sullenness. He had wished to return evil for evil. Now, however, evil had become his good. Not one more moment would he waste now before returning good for good. Could he succeed? He was in love; it did not follow that he was loved, or ever would be.

He never dreamed that Agatha could feel a deep respect for him – not only that, he mistook her feeling for aversion. His was a positive emotion, quite unlike that stubborn resistance masquerading as spirited independence that she had hitherto aroused in him. It was a total invasion of his being, a gnawing hunger that could not be appeased. It harried him incessantly, spurred him to take action . . . But what action? Never would he dare to speak his love. Besides, there would never be an opportunity. The formal pattern of their Faith, its schisms no less than its shared dogmas, made it well-nigh impossible to conduct a love affair; and so little did their public mode of life allow of private and particular communication, that even were he to bring himself to speak, she might not take him seriously.

A letter seemed the best solution. Fate had flung a pebble, the quiet pool was shaken; now, blindly, he would fling another, let it fall at random. He would drop his letter (special delivery) into the void, to take its chance. It would land secretly at the feet of Agatha; or in full view, and noisily; from one or other of these two alternatives the rest would follow logically.

He would conceal his agitation, pretend to retire for the evening in a fit of sulks, thus saving his face and achieving the necessary privacy for composition.

THE OUTCOME OF THIS stratagem was to exasperate Elisabeth and discourage poor Agatha entirely. She feared that Paul had turned against her and was deliberately avoiding her. Next day, she declared that she was ill, took to her bed, and refused to appear for the evening meal.

Elisabeth dined dismally *tête à tête* with Gérard. She then dismissed him, with instructions to get into Paul's room at all costs, work on him, force him to come clean. She herself, meanwhile, would look after Agatha.

She found her prostrate on her bed, in floods of tears, her head buried in the pillow. Elisabeth was beginning to look haggard. Some unquiet spirit was abroad, still faceless, but she sensed its threat in some unawakened layer of her spirit; some mystery, still nameless, but she could apprehend it. She was beside herself with anxious curiosity. Taking the unhappy creature in her arms, she rocked her on her breast and let her pour her heart out.

"I love him, I adore him," sobbed Agatha. "He doesn't care a rap for me."

So she was in love! . . . in love, of course, with Gérard. Elisabeth smiled.

"Silly girl," she said. "What makes you think he doesn't care a rap for you? Has he told you so? Of course not. Very well then. He doesn't know his luck, the silly ass! If you want him, you must marry him, he'll have to marry you."

Reassured, melted, anaesthetized by this undreamed-of outcome, by the simplicity of Elisabeth's acceptance where at best she had expected mockery, Agatha murmured:

"Lise," her face against this sisterly, this understanding bosom. "You are an angel. But I'm sure he doesn't love me."

"What makes you so sure?"

"He couldn't, not possibly."

"Gérard's awfully shy, you know," went on Elisabeth, still drenched with Agatha's tears, still rocking and consoling; when all of a sudden Agatha sat bolt upright.

"But . . . Lise . . . I didn't mean Gérard. I meant Paul!"

Elisabeth rose to her feet.

"Forgive me," stammered Agatha, "please forgive . . ."

Staring ahead of her, her arms slack along her sides, once more Elisabeth felt herself begin to heel, to founder. As once, before her eyes, her mother had become an unknown woman, dead, anonymous, so now the very mask of treachery confronted her instead of the known, tear-stained face of Agatha. A thief was in the house.

But she must control herself. She must know all. She came and sat down beside the bed.

[97]

"Paul! I'm staggered. I'd absolutely no idea . . ."

In honeyed tones she added:

"Well, how extraordinary! It seems so odd. It's staggering. Tell me all about it."

Once more she started to coax and cozen her, hoping to trap her into confidences and bring dark matters flocking to the light.

Agatha dried her eyes, blew her nose; she was only too ready to let herself be lulled once more into security. The floodgates were opened, and Elisabeth became the recipient of more hopes and longings, even, than the love-sick girl had ever dared inwardly avow.

Holding her clasped against her neck and shoulder, Paul's sister listened to the voice of love, of artless, boundless love. Had she, the speaker, but seen, so close above her, above the automatic hand stroking, stroking her hair, the graven face of adamantine justice, she would have been struck dumb.

Elisabeth stood up; said with a smile:

"Now listen. Just relax, don't worry. It's perfectly simple. I'm going to talk to Paul."

"No, no," cried Agatha, starting up in terror, "Paul must never guess! For God's sake, promise me you'll never breathe a hint . . ."

"Hush, darling, hush. You're in love with Paul. If he loves you back, everything's fine. I won't give you away, I promise you. I'll just sound him casually. I'll soon find out. You know you can trust me, go to sleep now. Don't budge from your room."

Elisabeth went down one flight of stairs. She was wearing a bathrobe fastened round the waist by a necktie. It was too long and got in her way. But she was walking, not of her own volition, but as if mechanically controlled, impelled to turn left, turn right, to open doors and close them with precision, without getting the hem of her bathrobe caught in her moving sandals. She felt she had become a robot, wound up to go through certain gestures; unless it went on going through its paces it would fall to pieces. Her heart thudded, heavy, dull, against her ribs, like an axe falling upon wood; there was a singing in her ears; her brain gave back no echo of her brisk forward march. Dreams resound sometimes with footsteps, mindless, purposeful, like hers; dreams lend us a gait lighter than winged flight, a step able to combine the statue's weight of inorganic marble with the subaqueous freedom of a deep-sea diver.

Hollow, leaden, buoyant, Elisabeth advanced along the corridor, her white wrap, billowing round her ankles, seeming to float her onward like a cloud: one of those foamy cloud-cushions devised by primitive painters to bear some Being of the angelic order. Only a faint humming persisted in her head; and in her breast nothing any more but an axe thudding out its mortal strokes.

From this time onward she was never to look back. The genius of the Room informed her utterly. She was possessed by it, as men of action – sea-captains, say, or financiers – in moments of supreme emergency may suddenly become possessed, and know by inspiration what act, what word, what gesture will save their ships and fortunes from the rocks; or as a criminal, in a blinding flash of intuition, lights on the one, the foolproof alibi certain to save him from the gallows.

Her feet brought her to the bottom of the little staircase leading to the gallery. Gérard appeared in the doorway.

"I was looking for you," he said. "Paul's in a very queer mood. He asked me to come and find you. How's the invalid?"

"She's got a sick headache, she's trying to get some sleep and doesn't want to be disturbed."

"I'll just look in on her."

"Don't. She's got to be kept quiet. Go to my room. Wait there till I come. I'm going to see Paul."

Secure in the knowledge of Gérard's unquestioning obedience, Elisabeth dismissed him and advanced into the room. For one moment the old Elisabeth shook off her cerements, took in the counterfeit before her of remembered moonlight, of remembered snow; the gleam of linoleum, the shadow shapes of furniture reflected in its polished surface; and in the centre, behind its high frail barricades, the sacred precincts of the Chinese city.

She walked all round them, pushed aside a panel in the screens, and found Paul sitting on the floor, his head and shoulders flung back against a pile of rugs. He was weeping. His tears were not like Agatha's; neither were they the tears he had shed once for ruined friendship. One after another they formed between his eyelids, swelled, brimmed over, trickled down his cheeks, collected near the corner of his lip, then fell again, slowly, drop after heavy drop.

The impact of his letter should have been violent. The letter could not have failed to reach Agatha. This vacuum, this suspense, was killing him, he could no longer bear the strain of self-control and silence. At all costs he must know, must be delivered from uncertainty. Elisabeth must be questioned; she had this moment come from Agatha.

"What letter?"

Had she not been forewarned, Elisabeth would doubtless have become provocative. In the ensuing slanging match, she might well have shown herself in her true colours; and Paul might well have held his tongue. But instead of a litigious adversary he found himself before a judge — a merciful judge; and he confessed. He poured out everything — his change of heart, his inability to deal with it, his letter written as a last resort — and begged Elisabeth to tell him whether or no Agatha was likely to reject his suit.

These successive depth-charges served only to set her automatically functioning upon another track. She was appalled to hear of the express letter. Suppose Agatha already had this trump card up her sleeve. . . . Suppose she had been playing it . . . Or had she put it aside unopened, then suddenly recognized the handwriting and torn it open? Was she opening it now, this very instant? Was she already on her way to Paul?

"Just a moment, my pet," she said. "Wait, I've got some important things to tell you. Agatha never said a word about your express letter. It can't have flown away. It's simply got to be found. I'm just going upstairs. I'll be back in no time."

She hurried away. Suddenly it struck her that the letter might still be in the hall: considered in retrospect, Agatha's despair seemed certainly authentic. No one had gone out. Gérard never bothered to look at the letters. If it had been left downstairs, it might still be there.

It was still there. The crumpled, dog-eared yellow envelope lay like a dead leaf on the salver.

She switched on the light. It was Paul's handwriting, a clumsy schoolboy scrawl, and the name on the envelope his own. Paul had written to himself! She tore it open.

This was a house devoid of writing paper; any odd scrap was used for scribbling messages. Paul had torn a page from an exercise book to write on. She unfolded it, and read:

Agatha, don't be angry. I love you. I was a fool. I thought you were my enemy. I've found out now that I love you and that if you don't love me, I shall die. I am on my knees, begging for an answer. I'm in agony. I shan't stir from the gallery.

Elisabeth shrugged her shoulders, grimaced contemptuously. Dashing down his own address, Paul, in his desperation, had mechanically prefixed it with his name as well. It was typical of him. He would never change.

Supposing this letter had come hurtling back to him like a boomerang, instead of lying impotent upon the table in the hall? He would have lost heart, lost hope, and, utterly humiliated by his own absent-mindedness destroyed it. She would spare him that.

She retired to the lavatory in the gentlemen's cloakroom, tore the letter into fragments, and pulled the plug on them.

Forthwith returning to her luckless brother, she told him that she had found Agatha fast asleep; adding that there was an express letter on the bedside table: she had seen it, a yellow envelope with a sheet of ruled paper sticking out of it. She had recognized it, because it was obviously one from the copybook on Paul's table.

"Didn't she even mention it when she was talking to you?"

"No, and I'd rather she never knew I'd seen it. And we must be particularly careful not to seem to be inquiring after it. She'd be sure to say she doesn't know what we're talking about."

Paul had never managed to envisage the actual consequences of his letter. Wishful thinking had inclined him towards optimism. What he had never expected was this abyss, this void. The tears streamed down his rigid face.

Elisabeth was prodigal of words of consolation, interspersing them with a minute account of a recent *tête à tête* with Agatha. The darling girl had broken down and told her all — how she loved Gérard, how he returned her love, how they intended to be married.

"It's odd," she persisted, "that Gérard hasn't said anything to you. I know he's afraid of me. I seem to scare him stiff. But it's different with you. I suppose he thought you wouldn't take it seriously."

Paul was dumb, drinking this inconceivable and bitter cup. Elisabeth continued to elaborate her theme. Paul must be mad! Agatha was a simple girl and Gérard was such a nice boy. They were made for one another. Gérard's uncle was getting old, Gérard would come into money, he would be free to marry Agatha and found a respectable bourgeois family. There seemed no impediment to their happiness. It would be monstrous, criminal, yes, criminal to throw a spanner, to cause trouble, to upset Agatha, to shatter Gérard, to poison both their futures. Paul could not, must not do it. It had been nothing but a passing fancy. When he thought it over, he would see for himself that a frivolous fancy such as his must yield to genuine and reciprocated love.

For a whole hour she went on talking, talking, delivering a lecture on his bounden duty. She felt herself inspired, launched on the flood of her own oratory. She sobbed. Paul bowed his head submissively, placed himself without reservation in her hands. He promised to hold his tongue and try to look cheerful when the young couple broke their news to him. It was clear from Agatha's silence that she had decided to forget about the letter, to make light of it, to forgive him. There might, of course, be a little awkwardness between them now: if Gérard noticed it would never do. But he and Agatha would have the wedding to look forward to — that would tide them over. In no time they would be off on their honeymoon, and bygones would be bygones.

Elisabeth dried Paul's tears, kissed him, tucked him up, and left him in his fortress. There was work to be done. The killer's instinct told her to strike blow on blow and never stop to think. Night-spinning spider, dexterous, deliberate, she went on her way, drawing her thread relentlessly behind her, hanging it to the four corners of the night.

She went to her own room, where she found Gérard expectantly hovering about.

"What's the news?" he asked eagerly.

She quelled him with a glance.

"How often have I told you not to yell? It's one of your worst habits. Well, the news is that Paul's ill. He hasn't got the sense to realize it. I know by his eyes, by his tongue. He's got a temperature. It's for the doctor to say whether it's a relapse or just a bout of 'flu.

Meanwhile, I've taken it upon myself to keep him in bed and not allow him any visitors. You can have the bed in his old room."

"No, I'd better be off."

"Don't go. I want to talk to you."

Her voice was ominous.

Bidding him be seated, she paced up and down in front of him, and presently inquired what he proposed to do about Agatha.

"Do what? Why?" he asked.

"What do you mean by 'why'?" And in harsh, cutting tones she told him he was not going to get away with it — he knew perfectly well that Agatha was in love with him, was expecting him to propose, and couldn't understand what he was playing at.

Gérard's jaw dropped. He stared at her dumbfounded.

"Agatha . . ." he stammered. "Agatha . . ."

"Yes, Agatha!" she blazed at him.

He really was a half-wit. His outings with Agatha should have given him a clue. And gradually she built up a picture of Agatha, not as a sisterly companion, but as a would-be wife, filling out the canvas with a wealth of dates and proofs, until Gérard was shaken to the core. She went on to say that Agatha was in great distress: she had got it into her head that Gérard was in love with her, Elisabeth, which was ridiculous, and anyway out of the question in view of her superior financial status.

Gérard longed for the ground to open and swallow him up. It cut him to the quick to hear her thus degrade herself — and him — with this uncharacteristic, this vulgar talk of money. She saw her advantage, seized it, and dealt him blow on mortal blow, forbade him

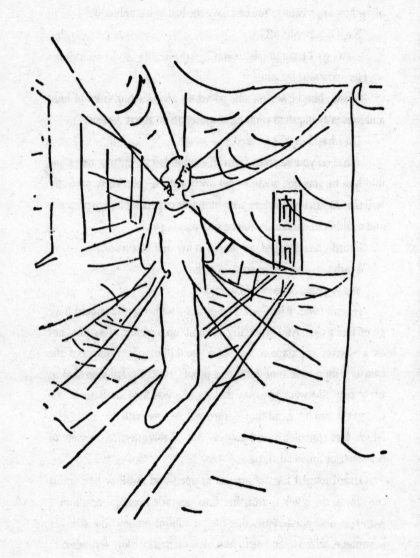

any more to pine for her, ordered him to marry Agatha and never to divulge her role of go-between. She had been forced into it by his obtuseness; and Agatha must never feel herself beholden to her for her married happiness — not for the whole world would she, Elisabeth, have that.

"Well, now," she concluded, "we've made a big step forward. Now go to bed. I'll just run up to Agatha and break it gently to her. You *are* in love with her. You've been living in a dream world. Your dreams carried you above your station. Wake up. Think how lucky you are. Give me a kiss and let me hear you say you're the happiest man alive."

Too stunned by now to offer any further resistance, Gérard bleated out some vague affirmation. She conducted him to Paul's room, and shut the door on him; then, sleepless Arachne, she climbed the stairs to Agatha.

MURDERERS HAVE BEEN KNOWN to find that young girls give them more trouble than anybody else.

Though Agatha reeled beneath the blows, she would not break. In the end, however, after a desperate battle, in the course of which Elisabeth went on insisting that Paul was incapable of love, that he did not love her because he could love no one; that self-destructive, monstrously selfish as he was, he could not fail to destroy any woman who surrendered to him; that Gérard, on the other hand, was that rare being, a man devoted and reliable enough to guarantee a woman's future happiness; in the end, the poor girl collapsed, worn out, and relinquished the last vestige of her dream. Prostrate beneath Elisabeth's scrutiny, she lay inert, uncovered, her head flung back, her damp hair sticking to her forehead, one hand pressed to her heart as if to staunch its wound, the other dropped stone-dead upon the floor.

Elisabeth raised her on her pillows, powdered her face, assured her that Paul was and would remain without an inkling of her feelings for him: all she had to do was to assume a cheerful face and tell him she was going to marry Gérard.

"Thank you . . . thank you . . . you are kind . . ." she gasped brokenly, between her sobs.

"Don't thank me, go to sleep," said Elisabeth; and left the room.

She paused for a second. She felt serene, detached, eased of a heavy burden. Just as she reached the stairs, her heart began to knock. She heard a footstep. A moment after, she saw Paul coming towards her.

His long white bathrobe made him luminous. In a flash she realized that he was walking in his sleep, as he had often done, when under strain, in the old rue Montmartre days. She leaned against the banisters, one foot suspended, not daring to move a muscle, lest Paul should wake and question her. But he did not see her where she stood palpitating, poised for flight; his gaze was on the stairs. She could have been a woman cast in bronze, holding a lamp to light his upward progress. The thudding axe of her heart sounded so loud in her own ears, she thought with dread that he must hear it too.

Paul stood still for a few moments, then turned away slowly and vanished into the silence. She stayed listening to his retreating steps, let fall her weight again on her numb foot, and stole away.

Back in her own room, she could hear nothing from next door. Was Gérard asleep? She stood long before the mirror in her bathroom. The image fascinated her. She bent her head; she washed her terrifying hands.

FEELING HIS END APPROACHING and anxious to see
the young couple settled as soon as possible, Gérard's uncle
hurried on the wedding preparations. The characters played their
allotted parts in an atmosphere of false cheerfulness and compet-
itive generosity. Behind the buzz and hum of cosy ritual lay the
mortal weight of the unspoken. The artificial merriment of Paul,
Agatha, and Gérard, weighed like lead upon Elisabeth's heart.
In vain she told herself that her vigilance had saved them all
from ship-wreck, that thanks to her Agatha would be preserved
from Paul and all his waywardness, and Paul from Agatha's medi-
ocrity. In vain she rehearsed her inward monologue: Gérard and
Agatha are two of a kind, they were bound to come together, we
were nothing but the intermediary, a year from now there'll be
a baby, they'll be blessing me. In vain she attempted to forget
her role of arbiter during the night of wrath, casting it from her
like a dream engendered by some cataleptic trance; in vain she
depersonalized the whole affair, dismissed it as the workings of
an all-seeing Providence: still she was troubled in the presence

of the melancholy trio, yet dared not leave them for fear of the dire consequences.

There was no one of them she did not trust. Could it ever have occurred to them to compare notes, they might have found reason to suspect her of malevolence, and forced her to a showdown; but they were too well-bred for that. Malevolent? But why? Why should she want to harm them? She was encouraged to find she could produce no answers. She loved them all, poor dears. They were her lifework, her vocation. She had gathered them beneath her wing, sheltered them, shouldered the entire burden of their follies, managed to avert the certain nemesis that would have overtaken them. She had paid, must pay, in blood and tears. It had to be.

She went on telling herself it had to be, in the manner of a surgeon staking his reputation on a crucial diagnosis. The dagger she had grasped became his scalpel. Confronted at a moment's notice with an acute emergency, she had had no option but to give the anaesthetic and perform the operation. Thanks to her skill, the patient was recovering. Then, at the sound of Agatha's strained laughter, at the sight of Paul's haggard face, of Gérard's artificial grin, she would start awake, beset once more by doubts and terrors, flying from the rumour of the chase behind her, knowing the Furies hard upon her heels.

The honeymoon left brother and sister alone together. Paul was pining visibly. Elisabeth moved in behind the barricades, sat up with him, nursed him day and night. The doctor was baffled by this mysterious relapse; but the whole illness had always been unorthodox. The bamboo hut dismayed him; he advised the removal of the patient to a comfortable room. Paul, permanently wrapped in a cocoon of shawls, refused to budge. A muffled light fell on the seated figure of Elisabeth, bowed forward, her chin propped in her hands, staring into space, careworn, consumed with sombre thoughts. As Gérard once, seeing the face of Paul flushed by the glory of the fire-engines, had fancied him reviving, so now she saw it bloom in the reflection from the scarlet bunting; and since false hopes were now her only diet, told herself it was, must be the ruddy glow of health.

The death of Gérard's uncle brought the young couple hurrying home. Elisabeth placed an entire floor of the mansion at their disposal; but despite her insistence they declined the offer, and took up residence in the rue Lafitte. This seemed to her to augur favourably for their future; they were clearly settling down contentedly to humdrum domesticity (the most they were entitled to) and had decided to shun their friends' unruly sphere of influence. When he heard of their decision, Paul breathed again. He had dreaded a resumption of their former intimacy.

"We're going to be dropped," declared Elisabeth. "We're thoroughly undesirable. Gérard made no bones about it. He says we're bad for Agatha. Yes, honestly! You wouldn't recognize him. He's turned into his uncle. I was absolutely staggered. At first I thought he had his tongue in his cheek. I thought he must be trying to get a rise out of me."

From time to time they came to the house for lunch or dinner.

Paul would leave his bed for the occasion and join the others in the dining-room. The meal would be swallowed to the accompaniment of brittle chatter, under the watchful eye of Mariette — the melancholy eye of a shrewd Breton; a peasant's eye for the shape of grief to come.

ONE DAY, JUST AS they were sitting down to lunch, Gérard said lightly:

"Guess who I ran into?"

Paul replied with an inquiring shrug.

"Dargelos!"

"Not really?"

"Yes, really, my dear fellow."

He went on to say that he had been almost run over by a small car when he was crossing the street. The car stopped: Dargelos was driving it. He had already heard that Gérard had inherited his uncle's property and was managing the factories. He was anxious to be shown over one. He obviously had an eye to the main chance.

Paul wanted to know if he had changed.

Pretty much the same, a bit less colour than he used to have . . . Extraordinarily like Agatha — might be taken for her brother. And quite the opposite of high-hat these days. Very, very friendly, in fact. He was an agent for a motor firm and spent his time travelling between France and Indo-China. He had taken Gérard back to

[117]

his hotel and asked him if he saw anything of Snowball . . . that snowball chap . . . he meant Paul.

"So what?"

"I told him I saw you constantly. Then he said: 'Does he still like poison?'"

Agatha gave a start.

"Poison?" she cried, thunderstruck.

"You bet." Paul's voice was loud, aggressive. "Glorious stuff, poison! I was always dying to get hold of some when I was at school." (It would have been more accurate to say that Dargelos was obsessed by poisons and that he, Paul, had copied Dargelos.)

"What could be the point?" asked Agatha.

"No point at all," said Paul. "Because I wanted it, I wanted to have some poison. It's glorious. I'd like to have it in the same way as I'd like to have a basilisk or a mandrake, in the same way that I like having a revolver. You've got it, you know you've got it, it's there for you to look at. It's poison. Glorious!"

Elisabeth agreed. It was an opportunity to snub Agatha and to demonstrate her old solidarity with the magic of the Room. She declared that she adored poison. In the days of the rue Montmartre, she used to play at brewing poisons, bottling and sealing them, sticking gruesome labels on them, making up sinister names.

"How ghastly! Gérard, they're mad! I know they'll end in jug."

Elisabeth was delighted by Agatha's outburst: by corroborating the bourgeois status she had conferred on the young couple, it absolved her of deliberate bad faith towards them. She caught Paul's eye and winked.

"Dargelos showed me his whole collection," went on Gérard. "Poisons from India, China, Mexico, the West Indies, poisons for arrow-tips, poisons for lingering death by torture, vendetta poisons, poisons for sacrificial rites. He said jokingly: 'Tell Snowball I haven't changed. I always wanted to collect poisons. Now I do so. Here, give him this to play with.'"

Under the goggling eyes of Elisabeth and Paul, Gérard felt in his pocket and pulled out a small package wrapped in a piece of newspaper. Agatha turned her back on the proceedings.

They opened the parcel, and found inside it a lump of something round and dark, about the size of a fist, contained in a flimsy paper sheath. It was the colour of earth, and had a texture not unlike a truffle, apart from one raw reddish gash in it. It gave off an odour as of clay newly dug; also a pungent whiff of onion and of oil of geranium.

Nobody spoke. They stood frozen before this object that drew and yet repelled them; as if a uniform reptilian mass should suddenly uncoil before their eye and rear a dozen snaky heads. It was death's absolute presence that confronted them.

"It's a drug," said Paul. "He must be a drug-addict. He wouldn't make so free with it if it was poison."

He put a hand out.

"Don't touch it!" Gérard pushed the hand away. "Whatever it is, it's a present from Dargelos, but he said you weren't on any account to touch it. But I wouldn't dream of letting you keep the beastly thing – you're much too casual."

Paul lost his temper. Taking his cue from Elisabeth, he told

Gérard not to be so stuffy. Who did he think he was? His dear departed uncle, etc.?

"Casual, are we?" sneered Elisabeth. "Just you wait!"

Snatching up the parcel, she started to chase her brother round and round the table, shouting:

"Go on, eat it, eat it!"

Agatha fled, Paul leapt on a table, buried his face in his hands. She panted after him, jeering: "There's a brave boy! See how casual he is!"

"Eat it yourself, you fool," retorted Paul.

"And die of it, I suppose. Suit you fine, wouldn't it? No, thanks, I propose to deposit *our* poison in the treasure."

"The smell's absolutely overpowering," said Gérard. "You ought to put it in a tin."

Elisabeth wrapped it up, shoved it into an empty biscuit tin, and vanished from the room. The top of the treasure chest was littered with their various possessions — revolver, books, the whiskered plaster bust; she opened a drawer, and placed the tin on top of Dargelos. Carefully, with infinite precautions, she set it down, with a schoolgirl's grimace of concentration; with something of the air, the gestures of a woman pricking a wax image, aiming precisely, then ramming home the pin.

Paul saw himself back at school again, aping Dargelos, obsessed with violence and barbaric rites, dreaming of poisoned arrows, hoping to impress his hero by an invention of his own, namely, a project for mass-murder by means of poisoned gum affixed to postage stamps. And all in wantonness, without a thought of poison's lethal implications, all to curry favour with a lout . . . Dargelos would shrug and turn away, scornful as of a silly girl.

Dargelos had not forgotten the abject slave who once hung on his lips: this gift of poison was the crowning stroke of his derision.

Its hidden promise filled the brother and sister with a strange elation. The Room had become richer by an extra, an incalculable dimension. It had acquired the potentials of an anarchist conspiracy; as if a charge of human dynamite had been sunk in it, would be touched off at the appointed hour, explode in blood sublimely, stream in the incandescent firmament of love.

Moreover, Paul was revelling in this parade of eccentricity from which Gérard, according to Elisabeth, wished to protect Agatha; it was a smack at Gérard and also at his wife.

Elisabeth, for her part, was triumphant. She saw the old Paul back upon the war path, trampling down convention, grasping the nettle danger, jealous as ever of the sacred treasure.

She invested the poison with symbolic properties: it was the antidote to pettiness and parochialism; would, must – surely – lead to the final overthrow of Agatha.

But Paul failed to respond to cure by witchcraft. His appetite did not improve; listless, apathetic, he went on pining, wasting, sinking by slow stages into a decline.

SUNDAY WAS A REGULAR day off for the whole household, according to the Anglo-Saxon custom adopted during
Michael's lifetime. Mariette filled the thermos flasks, cut sandwiches, then went out with the housemaid. The chauffeur, whose
duties included lending a hand indoors with the cleaning, borrowed
one of the cars and spent his time profitably, picking up casual
passengers for hire.

On this particular Sunday it was snowing. Acting on instructions
from the doctor, Elisabeth had gone to her own room to lie down and
had drawn the curtains. It was five o'clock. Paul had been dozing
since noon. He had insisted on her leaving him alone, had begged
her to listen to the doctor. She was asleep, and dreaming. She
dreamed that Paul was dead. She was walking through a forest, but
at the same time it was the gallery: she recognized it by the light
falling between the tree-trunks from tall windows set in dark
intermittent panels of opacity. She came to a furnished clearing
and saw the billiard-table, some chairs, one or two other tables.
She thought: I must get to the mound. In her dream she knew that

the word *mound* meant the billiard-table. Striding, sometimes skimming just above the ground, she made haste to reach it, but she could not. She lay down exhausted and fell asleep. Suddenly Paul roused her. She cried:

"Paul, oh Paul! So you're not dead?"

And Paul replied: "Yes, I am dead, but so are you. You've just died. That's why you can see me. You're going to live with me for ever and ever."

They went on walking. After a long time they reached the mound.

"Listen," said Paul, putting a finger on the automatic marker. "*Listen to the passing knell.*" The marker began to whirr dementedly. The glade began to hum louder, louder, a noise like buzzing telegraph wires . . .

She woke aghast, to find herself sitting bolt upright, drenched in perspiration. A bell was pealing. She remembered that the servants were all out. Still in the grip of nightmare, she ran downstairs and opened the front door. On a white whirlwind Agatha blew in, dishevelled, crying out: "Where's Paul?"

By now Elisabeth had come round, was shaking off the dream's last clinging threads.

"What do you mean?" she said. "What's the matter with you? Paul's asleep as usual, I suppose. He said he didn't want to be disturbed."

"Quick, quick," gasped Agatha, "run we must hurry. I had a letter, he said by the time I got it it would be too late, the poison, he'd have taken the poison, he said he was going to shut you out of his room and take it." She clutched Elisabeth, pushing, pulling, trying to urge her forward. Mariette had left a note at the young couple's flat at four o'clock.

Elisabeth stood stock still. It was the dream, she told herself, she must be still asleep. She was turned to stone. Then she was running. She and this other girl were running, running.

Now she had reached the gallery, but in the dream still, she was in a spectral glade of roaring wind and darkness, of trees whipped white in the interlucent spaces; and there, in the distance, still the *mound*, the billiard-table, the real and nightmare relic of an earthquake.

"Paul! Paul! Speak to us! Paul!"

There was no answer. The shining precincts gave back, for all reply, a charnel breath. They broke in; and the full impact of the disaster hit them simultaneously. The Room was thick with an ominous aroma: they knew it — reddish, black, a compound of truffles, onions, essence of geranium, overpowering, beginning already to invade the gallery. His eyeballs starting from their sockets, his face distorted beyond recognition, Paul lay supine, wearing a bathrobe exactly like his sister's. Lamplight, snow-blurred, eddying down through the high windows, threw gusts of shifting shadow across the livid mask, touched nose and cheekbones into faint relief. Beside him on the chair, jostling one another, lay the remainder of the poison, a water bottle, and the photograph of Dargelos.

The actual tragedies of life bear no relation to one's preconceived ideas. In the event, one is always bewildered by their simplicity, their grandeur of design, and by that element of the bizarre which seems inherent in them. What the girls found impossible, at first was to suspend their natural disbelief. They had to admit to accept the inadmissible, to recognize this unknown shape as Paul.

Rushing forward, Agatha flung herself on her knees beside him, brought her face close to his, discovered he was breathing. A flicker of hope leapt up in her.

"Lise," she urged, "don't stand there doing nothing, go and get dressed, he may be only doped, this frightful thing may not be deadly poison. Get a thermos flask, run and fetch the doctor."

"The doctor's away, he's shooting this week-end," stammered the wretched girl. "There's nobody . . . there's nobody . . ."

"Quick, quick, get a thermos! He's breathing, he's icy cold. He must have a hot water bottle, we must get some hot coffee down his throat."

Agatha's presence of mind amazed Elisabeth. How could she bring herself to speak, touch Paul, how could she so bestir herself? How did she know he needed a hot water bottle? What made her think she could prevail by common sense against the implacable decrees of snow and death?

Abruptly she pulled herself together, remembered that the thermos flasks were in her bedroom. She flew to get them, calling over her shoulder:

"Cover him up!"

Paul was still breathing. Since swallowing what Dargelos had sent him, he had endured four hours of sensations so phenomenal that he had wondered intermittently whether the stuff was after all a drug, not poison, and if so, whether he had taken a sufficient dose to

kill him; but now the worst of the ordeal was over. His limbs had ceased to exist. He was floating in space, had almost recaptured his old sense of well-being. But his saliva had entirely ceased to flow, and consequently his dry tongue rasped his throat like sandpaper; except where all feeling had become extinct, his parched skin crawled unbearably. He had attempted to drink. He had put a faltering hand out, groping in vain to find the water bottle. But now his legs and arms were all but paralysed; and he had ceased to move.

Whenever he closed his eyes, the same images reappeared: the head of a giant ram with a woman's long grey locks; some dead and blinded soldiers marching in stiff military procession, slowly, then faster, faster, round and round a grove: he saw that their feet were tethered to the branches. The bedsprings shook and twanged beneath him to the wild knocking of his heart. The veins swelled, stiffened in his arms, the bark grew round them, his arms became the branches of a tree. The soldiers circled round his arms; and the whole thing began again.

He sank into a swoon, was back in the time of snow, the old days of the Game, was in the cab with Gérard driving home. He heard Agatha sobbing:

"Paul! Paul! Open your eyes, speak to me . . ."

His mouth felt clogged with sourness. His gummed-up, flaccid lips framed one word only: "Drink . . ."

"Try to be patient . . . Elisabeth has gone to get the thermos. She's bringing a hot water bottle."

"Drink . . ." he said again.

Agatha moistened his lips with water. She took his letter from her handbag, showed it to him, begged him to try and tell her what madness had come over him.

"It's your fault, Agatha."

"My fault?"

Syllable by syllable, he started to whisper, stammer out the truth. She interrupted him with protestations, exclamations. The man-trap was exposed in all its tortuous ingenuity. Together the dying man and the young woman touched it and turned it over, unscrewed the diabolical contrivance piece by piece. Their words engendered a stubborn, treacherous, criminal Elisabeth, whose machinations of that night were plain at last.

"You mustn't die!" cried Agatha.

"Too late," he mourned.

At that moment, Elisabeth, fearful of leaving them too long alone together, came hurrying back with the thermos and the hot water bottle. There was a moment of unearthly silence; then nothing but the pervasive smell of death again. Elisabeth had her back turned, she was busy hunting among boxes and bottles, looking for a tumbler, filling it with coffee, not yet aware that all had been discovered. She advanced towards her victims, saw they were watching her, stopped dead. By a savage and supreme effort, with Agatha's arms round him, her cheek against his cheek, Paul had half-raised himself among the pillows. Deadly hatred blazed from both their faces. She held the coffee out towards him, but a cry from Agatha arrested her:

"Paul, don't touch it!"

"You're mad," she muttered, "I'm not trying to poison him."

"I wouldn't put it past you."

This was more than death, it was the heart's death. Elisabeth swayed on her feet. She opened her mouth, but no words came.

"Devil! Foul devil!"

His words confirmed the worst of her suspicions and crushed her with an extra weight of horror: she had not dreamed he had the strength to speak.

"Foul, filthy devil!"

Over and over again, with his dying breath, he spat it at her, raking her with his blue gaze, with a last long volley of fire from the blue slits between his eyelids. His lips, that had been so beautiful, twisted and spasmodically; from the dried well of what had been his heart rose nothing but a tearless glitter, a wolfish phosphorescence.

The blizzard went on battering at the windows. Elisabeth flinched, then said:

"Yes, you're right, it's true. I was jealous. I didn't want to lose you. I loathe Agatha. I wasn't going to let her take you away."

Stripped, her disguise thrown off at last, she took the truth for garment, she grew in stature. As if blown by a storm, her locks streamed back and her small fierce brow loomed monumental, abstract, above the lucent eyes. She stood fast by the Room, she stood against them all, defying Agatha, Gérard, Paul, and the whole world.

She snatched up the revolver from the chest of drawers.

"She's going to shoot! She's going to kill me!" screamed Agatha. She clung to Paul but he had left her side, was wandering.

Elisabeth had no thoughts of making Agatha her target. She had seized the revolver, not to shoot down this elegant flesh-and-blood young woman, but with the last gesture of the spy unmasked, her

back against the wall, her supreme instinct a determination to sell her life as dearly as she could.

But the gesture was lost on such an audience. What could it avail to put on greatness for a dying man and a hysterical young woman?

So this is what Agatha saw suddenly: a maniac in the act of disintegrating before her very eyes, standing before the mirror, mopping and mowing, drooling, squinting, tearing her hair out by the roots. For Elisabeth had given up: no longer able to bear this slackening in the pace of nemesis, she was trying to resolve her inner tension by letting herself collapse, was struggling by means of this grotesque mime of imbecility to reduce life to its ultimate absurdity, to push back the frontiers of what might still have to be endured, to attain the moment when the drama would have done with her at last, would spew her forth.

"She's gone mad! Help! Help!" screamed Agatha.

The word "mad" acted as a check upon Elisabeth; with an effort, she controlled herself. She would be calm now. She had two weapons — death and oblivion — in her trembling hands. With her head bowed, she stood erect.

She knew that the Room was rushing headlong down a giddy slope towards its end; but the end was not yet, and must be lived through: there must be no slackening of the tension. Snatches of the multiplication table went whirling through her head, odds and ends of figures, dates, street numbers: she added them all together, divided them, made nonsense of them, started all over again. Suddenly she remembered the origin of the *mound*: "mound" was the word for "hill" in *Paul et Virginie*. Their island . . . Where could it have been?

The Île de France? The names of islands began to float across her mind. Île de France, Mauritius; Île Saint Louis. She recited the names, transposed them, shuffled them, annulled them, created void at last, achieved the vortex.

Paul felt the impact of her utter calm. He opened his eyes. She looked at him, encountered a remote yet dwelling gaze, emptied of hatred now, beginning to deepen secretly with curiosity. She saw, and felt a premonitory surge of triumph, knew that the knot that bound them still held fast. Fixing her eyes unswervingly on his, spinning out the thread of trance towards him, adding and subtracting automatically, making lists of names and places, slowly she spread the net around him, surely she drew him backward into nothingness, back into the Game, into their world of light air, their Room.

With the preternatural clairvoyance of fever, she penetrated into the most secret places. The shades obeyed her. What hitherto she had wrought mindlessly, building as bees build, no more aware of motive or direction than a patient in a deep hypnotic sleep, she now created and directed consciously. Like one who under sudden violent shock rises from long paralysis and walks, she moved, she took her bearings.

She was drawing Paul, and Paul was following her: no doubt of it. Certainty was the rock on which she based her mental structure. She piped, she piped, she charmed him, he swayed to her tune. Already, she knew it, he no longer felt Agatha clinging round his neck; he had already become deaf to her laments. How should Elisabeth or Paul have heard her? Her cries are pitched far below the key they have selected for their requiem. Now they ascend, together they ascend. Elisabeth bears away her prey. They don the buskins of the Attic stage and leave the underworld of the Atrides behind them. Divine omniscience will not suffice to shrive them; they must put their trust in the divine caprice of the Immortals. Courage, one little moment longer and they will be where flesh dissolves, where souls embrace, where incest lurks no more.

Agatha's screams resounded from another time, another place. To Elisabeth and Paul they were of less significance than the majestic blizzard knocking on the windows. Dusk had retreated before the lamp's harsh glare; Elisabeth alone remained beyond its radius, within the shadow of its blood-red kerchief, cloaked in its purple, spinning the void, drawing Paul over the border from the realms of light into the realms of darkness.

He was sinking. He was ebbing out towards Elisabeth, towards the snow, the Game, the Room, their childhood. Still by a single thread of light the Maiden Goddess holds him out of darkness; his stone body is still penetrated by one last all-pervading thought of life. Still his eyes held his sister; but she was nothing more than a tall shape without identity, calling his name. For still, her finger on the trigger, like one clasped with her lover in the act of love, Elisabeth watched and waited on his pleasure, cried out to him to hasten to his mortal spasm, to accompany her into the final moment of mutual rapture and possession, mutual death.

Now he was spent, his head fell back. She thought the end had come, put the revolver to her temple, pulled the trigger. With a roaring din, one of the screens crashed on her as she fell. The

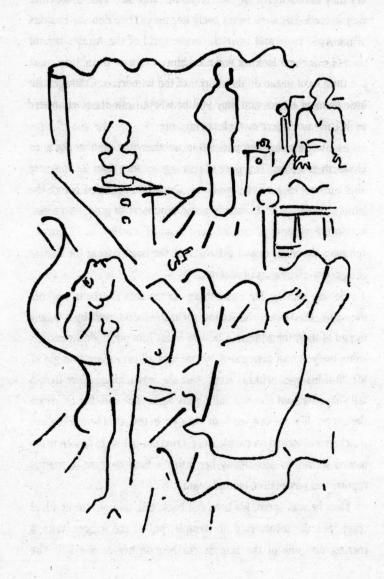

walls were breached, the secret shrine exposed, raw, violated, a public spectacle, to the eyes watching Paul in the snow-shrouded windows.

He saw them looking down on him.

While Agatha stood dumb, transfixed with terror, staring at the bloodstained corpse that was Elisabeth, Paul saw them, splintered in the frosty panes, saw, thronging, pressing in, the snowballers, their noses, cheeks, red hands. He recognized their features, their capes, their woollen mufflers. He looked for Dargelos and could not find him; all he could see was that one vast gesture of Dargelos's lifted arm.

"Paul! Paul! Help! Help!"

But who is she to call upon his name? What part or lot has she in him? His eyes are quenched. The thread is broken. The Room has flown; all that remains is the foul breath of poison, and one small stranded figure, the figure of some woman, dwindling, fading, disappearing in the distance.

www.vintage-classics.info